THE FUNERAL

THE FUNERAL

HELEN H. DURRANT

bookouture

Published by Bookouture in 2025

An imprint of Storyfire Ltd.
Carmelite House
50 Victoria Embankment
London EC4Y 0DZ

www.bookouture.com

The authorised representative in the EEA is Hachette Ireland
8 Castlecourt Centre
Dublin 15 D15 XTP3
Ireland
(email: info@hbgi.ie)

ISBN: 978-1-83525-953-5
eBook ISBN: 978-1-83525-952-8

For my daughter Melissa, whose help with so many things while I've been writing this book has been invaluable.

ONE

For the last three years, I've avoided people for fear of being recognised, but today all that will change. I've been invited to a funeral, but if I had a choice in the matter, I'd be spending my day off doing something less sombre, like a trip round the shops or tea out somewhere nice. Who am I kidding? That costs money and I haven't got any. Which is why I'm here today, why I've risked breaking cover. It's far enough away from where I live that no one is likely to know me anyway. Fingers crossed.

Usually at these occasions, the deceased is someone you know well, but not this time. The invite came by email, unusual because I live under the radar and haven't used that email address in months. I can count on the fingers of one hand the people who know it. Anonymous, and with no clue who sent it, not even the name of the deceased, I thought it might be some sort of scam. I replied and asked for more information but my reply bounced back.

I've been through a lot in life, so I know to be careful. The email is suspicious; what I should have done is delete it, but I didn't and for one reason only. The mysterious sender said that the deceased had been fond of me and that I'd been left something – money, I hope. The temptation of enough money to start my life again is so strong that I'm prepared to finally come out of hiding.

I've been living on my small amount of savings, which has now gone, and cash in hand from the local shop where I get the odd night shift. The hours are long, the customers barely look at me and don't want conversation, which suits me. My safety depends on as few people as possible recognising me or knowing where I am.

I borrowed money, not a great amount, but I couldn't keep up the repayments. With the added interest, the loan grew to an amount I stood no chance of ever paying back. I didn't know what to do, the lender has a bad reputation. I was afraid and made the decision to move to a different part of Manchester where no one knows me.

Since the email hit my inbox, I've thought long and hard about what to do. At first I thought the man I borrowed money from had found me. I don't own a laptop so I use an internet café. I'm looking for another bedsit and have just started checking *for rent* ads. I'd logged on and had been about to take a bite of the sandwich I'd made for lunch when I saw it. Given that other people use this laptop I thought it had to be a mistake. But I was wrong; the email was definitely meant for me. Logic tells me that it can't have anything to do with my past. I've not seen or heard from anyone in three years and the rumour mill is silent. That fact and the prospect of money are the reasons I've thrown caution to the wind and why I'm picking my way carefully over a patch of rough ground towards the graveside of someone I didn't know.

Now that I'm here, that little voice in my head is telling me this is not a good idea.

I'm getting closer to the group of mourners around the grave; this is panic time. I'm no good at making small talk with a crowd of strangers. Looking at the expensive clothes on their backs and the flashy cars in the car park, I certainly don't fit in. It would be stupid to wimp out now; I've worked hard all week preparing for this. Given my lack of money, my outfit is from a charity shop. Nothing wrong with that, especially as the dress I bought is a good make and fits well. The jacket is another matter. The sleeves are on the long side and there is a small stain on one of the pockets. Its saving grace is that it goes beautifully with the dress.

As I glance down at my outfit, I have to admit that I don't look half bad. The letdown is the oversized shoes on my feet. I tried to make them fit by stuffing toilet roll into the toes but that just makes them hurt. I saw the pair of black stilettos in a charity shop window. It's been such a long time since I wore anything like them, but I couldn't resist. Prancing around with these on my feet reminds me of times long gone, back when I was the old me, a happier me altogether. But I haven't had time to practise wearing the shoes, an omission with consequences. Within minutes of joining the others, I trip over a tree root and go flying. I land front down, doing heaven knows what damage to both me and the clothes in the process.

Anxiety makes me clumsy, two left feet, my aunt Nancy used to say. Not as a criticism, more in fondness, in a 'you wouldn't be you without them' sort of way. In the depths of the night, when I'm alone, I think of Nancy and shed a tear. She was the only member of my family who had any time for me. Sometimes when I think of her, I imagine I smell violets, the same as the perfume she always wore.

It's my knees that take the brunt of the fall, and when I look down I see shredded tights and a nasty graze. This is a disaster just when I didn't need one. I'm shaking with both nerves and shock; both will eat away at my confidence and make me even more tongue-tied than usual. If anything was going to let me down, I knew it would be the shoes. They are an indulgence too far.

Picking myself up I check if anyone has seen. Fortunately the other guests are stood by the grave, their faces too intent on the vicar to notice me. This had better be worth it, I think, as I limp forward.

To make matters worse, I'm late too, but there's nothing I can do about that either. The funeral is a long way from where I live and it took me hours on public transport to get here. It was wishful thinking to imagine the bus would turn up on time. As I'd watched the Cheshire countryside pass by, I knew I was never going to make the service, but I'd come this far, so there was no turning back.

People I don't know are gathered by the graveside. I just know this will be embarrassing. Fingers crossed that I don't make a show of myself.

I join the small gathering. Not wanting to intrude, I stand at the back of the group. The email said I'd been a friend to this person. Perhaps I had, but looking around I'm now doubly sure that there has been a mistake. For a start, I don't know anyone here. If me and the deceased had been friends, I would expect to recognise somebody.

This is a mix-up; it has to be. These people know each other, the nods tell me that much. They're wealthy; the way they're dressed shouts money. My life is as far removed from this lot as one can get. My wardrobe is non-existent and what few mates I have are all stony-broke like me.

People move forward to listen to the vicar do his final bit. Directly behind me a woman tuts with disapproval. I overhear her ask the woman stood next to her who I am.

'Some chancer, Isabel. Has to be, look how she's dressed,' is the reply.

I want to turn around, ask why she's being so rude to me, but my attention is on the trickle of blood that's now running down my leg from the fall. She sees it too, sticks her nose in the air, but doesn't come forward to help. That is left to a tall, handsome man in a dark suit. He stands beside me, smiles and hands me a tissue. I give him a nod of thanks. He's a welcome ally just when I need one.

'Take no notice of those two. They're only here for the food and the gossip at the wake,' he says. 'You'll be upset.' He nods at the grave. 'Was she your friend?'

Friend? The truth is I've no idea. I decide not to say anything. I'm on shaky ground as it is. At least I now know whoever they're burying is a *she*. Shame I know nothing else about the woman. Her name would be helpful.

'This one will be after something, mark my words.' More vitriol comes from behind, aimed at me. 'I mean, look at her, she's got all the style of an alley cat and probably the manners to match.'

I turn and take a closer look at her. She's a stranger, a woman in her thirties, tall, elegant with dark mid-length hair and a tan that speaks of holidays in the sun. I haven't the foggiest why she's so dead set against me. And she's wrong, I'm after nothing. Well, I'm not sure what I'm after just yet. I don't even know who's in the coffin.

'Shut it, Isabel,' the suit barks at her. 'This young lady is grieving too.'

He's mistaken but it's better to keep the truth to myself for now. I check my mobile for the email and have a quick read. This situation is so bizarre; I have to be at the wrong funeral. But I'm not; it's all there. I've been given the time and place and instructed to accompany the family to the wake afterwards. I haven't got a clue what's going on. I should walk away, get the next bus to my neck of the woods and not look back.

Little do I know now that within the next few days I'd wish I'd done just that...

I hear more tutting then the one called Isabel yanks the suit's arm from my shoulder. It's obvious to me that this intimate little interlude with him hasn't gone down well. I've caused a stir at this sad family event and, for reasons I can't fathom, one of the party hates me on sight. Perhaps others do to, I just don't know. Standing here, I feel sorry for whoever they've buried. Living among this lot can't have made her happy.

I give the suit a smile of thanks and walk forward. Call it my sense of the macabre but I'm curious. The only other funeral I've been to was that of a friend who'd been living rough. I tried to help him but got nowhere. I would have taken him in myself but I was sofa-surfing and living in a friend's bedsit at the time. The entire incident was sad and affected me for a long time afterwards. Tommy had died alone in a cold, wet doorway. That shouldn't happen to anyone, not in this day and age.

He'd been cremated, a sad affair with few mourners, and there wasn't much to see. The people here today live in an entirely different world. This woman's friends and family can afford flowers and a wake to follow. Between all the people who'd known Tommy, we could do nothing like this for him.

A burial is different from a cremation. It's much more horrific to see a coffin being slowly lowered into a hole in the ground. The pile of earth by its side makes me shudder. Soon, it will cover the lot, leaving the coffin and the body for the worms and other creepy crawlies to feast on. The finality of it all sends a shiver down my spine.

The vicar has finished, and people are moving away. Stuff the wake, I won't be missed anyway; I'm not one of their kind. But I still don't know the name of the deceased. In case anyone asks, and to quench my own curiosity, I'll find out. I move nearer to the grave and take one last look as the coffin is lowered and buried forever.

That is a big mistake.

I'm certain now that inviting me here today is no accident. I am the star attraction. Etched on the gold plaque adorning the pristine white coffin, and in large letters, is *Alice Anderson.*

My name.

TWO

'You've gone pale. Are you alright?'

Alright is a long, long way from how I feel right now. I've just had the shock of my life.

I've attended my own funeral.

I imagine all sorts as I try to think who could possibly be responsible for this. The man I owe money to is a candidate but only if he has found out my new name, but how likely is that? I've been careful, made sure I have no links with my old life.

The sound of the male voice snaps me back to reality. It's deep, sexy and I've heard it before. It's the suit.

I turn and look at him. I desperately want to tell someone, have them explain to me what just happened, but my instinct tells me to hold back. Why, I can't fathom, because at this moment I need all the reassurance I can get that I'm not mad.

Perhaps he can help me. Instinct aside, I'm tempted to tell him. He seems a kind man, the type who'd try his best to sort any problem for you. Perhaps he can help me find out who invited me here and why the deceased has my name. Seeing it on that coffin has freaked me out, scared the life out of me, and I don't scare easily.

'The wake is at the house where Alice lived. I can give you a lift if you want.'

His face breaks into a smile, and for the first time I take a proper look at him. Tall, broad shoulders and with the sort of face that could easily lead a girl astray. Is he single? Mad idea. I give myself a mental shake. These are alien thoughts for me. Given my experience in the past, I gave up on men a long time ago, plus I have more important things to think about.

'That will be great, thanks,' I say. 'I don't have an address.' Stupid thing to say. If I knew the woman well enough to attend her funeral, why not? I avoid his eyes. Any minute now it'll be him firing the questions, like who I am, what was my relationship to the deceased woman. Thankfully I'm wrong, and instead, he apologises for the barracking from the two women earlier.

'I'm sorry you had to endure those jibes from Isabel and her friend. She has a sharp tongue and doesn't know when to curb it.' I get a comforting nod and respond in kind. 'I'm Max Marsden, Alice's employer until she died. This sad little do is down to me. Alice had no one else in the world; well, no one else that we knew about,' he says. 'For the last two years she worked as my office assistant and at times as my PA, so I thought it the least I could do.'

'Very kind of you,' I reply.

The fact she had no one else is interesting but near the bottom of my list of questions. Far more important is why she'd used my name and how she knew me.

'You will come back to the house? Alice lived in with us, so it was her home too – a perk of the job.'

Lucky Alice; I wish I could get a job like that.

'We've planned a small send-off, food etc. After this morning, I could do with a stiff drink.'

Me too.

'Was Alice a friend of yours, or perhaps a relative?'

Here we go with the tricky questions, and I don't blame him. I turn up out of the blue, looking totally out of place, and say I knew the dead woman. He must have his doubts; as far as he knew, Alice had no one, friend or family.

'She was a friend,' I reply, hoping that will be the end of it. I'm in no mood for questions; I've got too many of my own.

'Alice rarely spoke of her life before she worked for me, and no one ever came to visit her. I did suggest she contact her friends and family, invite them round, but she never did. We'd begun to think she was all alone in the world but here you are to disprove that.'

I shrug, while thinking of an explanation. 'We lost touch, and I haven't seen her in a while. I suppose I should have phoned but she dropped out of my life.'

He nods, and I breathe a sigh of relief that he accepts this.

'And you are?'

I can't dodge this one.

'Donna Slade.' I smile again.

It's a lie but I can hardly tell him my real name, that the woman he's just buried stole mine, so I've had to steal a new one. Not strictly true. I did steal the name, but it had nothing to do with the dead woman.

I've been using *Donna* for the last three years, ever since I ran away. To stay anonymous, a new name was a necessity. Not that the real Donna Slade will bother about any of that. I found notice of her death on social media. I've no idea why I chose it, but the name appealed to me, and of course no one will come looking. So Alice Anderson became Donna Slade, the perfect solution.

'Perhaps she mentioned me?' I ask him.

I know very well that's not possible but whatever I say must sound plausible.

'She may have mentioned your name but, to be honest, I can't be sure. I take it you found out about the funeral from the announcement we put in the local and Manchester papers.'

For the time being I'll avoid that question and ask one of my own. 'How did Alice die?'

'An accident,' came his reply. 'Tragic and avoidable, but isn't that the way of all accidents?'

I'm not sure, but I want to know more; perhaps later I'll have the opportunity to ask again. But I've found out that he doesn't know about the email. That means it wasn't him who sent it. I feel relieved, which is illogical because there's no reason it couldn't have been him. If this is what a good-looking man does to my brain, what chance do I have of finding out the truth.

Max Marsden guides me towards the cars in the car park and points to a sleek sports job.

'I'd better find my wife. She'll have found someone to gossip to; if I don't tear her away we could be here all afternoon,' he jokes. 'I'll open the car door for you then go and see where she's got to.'

Wife, that's a shame. I stifle the inappropriate thoughts I have about him. Of course he has a wife. He's a dish of a man; it would be odd if he hadn't been snapped up.

He holds one of the rear doors open and I clamber in. The smell of leather and expensive perfume hits me straight away. A ride in a posh car like this is a new experience for me. Something else that shouts money; in fact, everything about this area does. The quaint cottages and houses in the small villages the bus has passed through on the way here. They looked as if they'd come straight off a Christmas card with one of those old-fashioned scenes on the front. I'm deep in the Cheshire countryside, light years away from Manchester city centre. I'm rarely jealous – I accept my lot for what it is – but what I wouldn't give to live around here.

Max Marsden is gone about five minutes and returns with a

woman gripping his arm so hard it looks as if she's in danger of tearing it off.

As he helps her into the car, he says nothing; it's left to her to do the introductions.

'I'm Tara, Max's wife.'

Short and sweet. She sits next to me in the back, making me feel totally inadequate. She's as gorgeous as him and doesn't she know it. Ignoring me, she takes a small mirror from her bag, her eyes fixed on her reflection while she runs perfectly manicured nails through her chin-length blonde hair.

I try to analyse the tone of her voice and her body language, not that I'm any sort of expert. Is she friendly or the jealous type? Mind you, her being jealous of me is a ridiculous idea.

'And you are?' she asks, with her face still fixed on the mirror.

Here we go, the tricky bit. I wince and cross my fingers. She must believe this. 'Donna Slade.'

'Well, Donna Slade, how did you know our Alice?'

She puts the mirror away and gives me her complete attention. 'I didn't know her well, but she did me a huge favour a while ago. I felt it only right to be here today.'

What have I said? Not engaged my brain, that's for sure. This could lead to more questions I don't have answers for. I could have said anything, that we'd met at the hairdressers or the shops, but no, I had to invent a *favour*.

'That sounds like Alice, doesn't it, Max? Kind to a fault.'

She taps Max on the shoulder. 'Hanna rang, she said the caterers arrived at the house on time and have set everything up. If they do a good job, perhaps we should book them for our anniversary.'

The nerves are back; there were only a small number of mourners at the graveside, but to me, *caterers* mean quite a crowd. I should have left after the service and made some excuse about the wake. I could be walking into a trap.

Someone invited me here today and they know me as *Donna*. That person has to be someone I know. A shiver of fear slips down my spine and I go cold. Has my past finally found me, found out my new name? Is it possible that they know the Marsdens?

Tara flicks the curtain of blonde hair off her face and looks me up and down. 'You're not local, that much is obvious.'

My back stiffens; here's someone else with no qualms about being rude. My clothes aren't new or particularly fashionable but there's no need for a comment like that. Now I feel awkward. This is an upmarket part of Cheshire and, fair enough, someone like me doesn't fit in. There is no hiding that my clothes are from a charity shop, that they fit badly or that my accent is very *Manchester*.

'I'm from Longsight,' is my reply.

'Near the city centre?'

I nod, wondering what she thinks of that. From the look on her face, not much.

I half expect another derisive comment, but with a sudden change of attitude she gives me a sympathetic smile. 'Very different from leafy Cheshire,' she nods. 'I hope you enjoy your day away from the city.'

'For pity's sake, Tara,' Max snaps at her, 'it's a funeral, not a day out. What's to enjoy at an occasion like this.'

Her expression hardens and those big blue eyes narrow.

'There's no need to shout, Max. I didn't mean anything by it. I'm upset, that's all. I find burials particularly difficult to witness.'

Me too, but I say nothing.

'Look, I know you're upset; we all are. Take no notice of the short temper. I'm having difficulty imagining life without our Alice,' Max tells his wife.

She pats his shoulder. 'I know, I'll miss her too.'

Whoever 'their' Alice was, she was important to them.

Important to me too, I reckon. I just wish I knew who she was and why she had my name.

'Perhaps we should take time off, go away to somewhere warm. Alice told me that you're doing too much, letting the business get on top of you.'

Tara spoke to him softly; she's a woman trying to help. But Max isn't in the mood for advice. I can see his face in the rear-view mirror.

'Don't tell me what to do, Tara,' he wearily replies. 'Down-time, as you put it, is not possible just now. Perhaps in a few weeks.'

'I'm only thinking of you. The business won't suffer if you're not at the helm for a few days.'

'How things are with the business and whether I can leave it isn't up to you. What would really help, Tara, is getting you off my back.'

'Okay, you obviously know best,' Tara sniffs. 'Things will be difficult with no Alice around. You should try and pace yourself. It could be a while before we find a replacement.'

'Replacement! She wasn't a light bulb, Tara. She was my right arm; she knew the business every bit as well as I do.'

Tara turns and looks at me again.

'He's a workaholic, never stops,' she whispers. 'I keep warning him, telling him that it will eventually have consequences, but he takes no notice.'

Despite the whispering, he heard that.

'If I listened to my wife, the business would go under.' Catching my eye in the mirror, he smiles.

'I worry about you, Max. I don't want to upset you, only to help.'

'I know you do, sweetheart,' he sighs. 'I'm a bad-tempered idiot at times and I'm sorry. We don't usually behave like this, Donna, but Alice's death has hit us both hard. Emotions are running high, especially today.'

Tara pats my hand, looks me in the face and mouths, *sorry*. 'Do you have anyone in your life, Donna?' she asks, changing the subject round to me.

I shake my head. There's been no one in my life for a long time and there's unlikely to be. Not that I want to tell Tara that. It makes me sound sad.

'I wouldn't worry. You're a lovely young woman; the right man will come along sooner or later.'

I don't feel lovely. I have long red hair that never lays flat; it's always stuck up at funny angles. As a child I was called names, made to feel odd because of it. It's so long since I visited a hairdresser's that now it's halfway down my back and more often than not tied back in a ponytail. I don't possess any make-up, fancy face creams and I'm too thin. I shake my head. 'I'm not looking for a relationship,' I assure her.

The reply is a high-pitched laugh that reminds me of those wind chimes people hang in their gardens.

'All women want a man in their lives,' she tells me with certainty. 'It's how we're made. Take my advice, Donna, don't be too quick to rule men out of your life.'

'You're embarrassing the poor woman,' Max interrupts. 'Today isn't the right time to be discussing Donna's love life.' He winks at my reflection in the mirror.

'Just small talk, Max,' she replies.

I've no intention of telling her, but the truth is right now I'm not interested in having a man in my life or what I look like. Keeping fed and warm will do me. But I do have dreams: 'wild, never in a million years will they happen' sort of dreams. A loving husband, our own home and children. Now I have a lump in my throat. A husband one day, but a child? I have no right to even think of wanting one.

I dab at my knee with a tissue. It's still bleeding, and I'll feel awful if I drip blood all over the expensive leather upholstery.

'A few minutes more and we'll be at the house, then I'll sort that cut properly,' Tara says, looking at the graze. 'We don't want it getting infected.'

I'm not bothered about my leg; I'm more bothered about the wake. Having to mix with strangers is terrifying for me. I've not been to any social occasion in such a long time, I've forgotten how to interact with people. Having questions is all very well but how can I possibly get the answers mixing with a room full of strangers?

I'm overthinking it, looking for problems that aren't there. Get on with what you came here to do, find out what you can about the deceased then get the hell out of here.

I scrutinise Tara's face for any sign that I'm in danger. I can't think why that popped into my mind but it did. The email... the name on the coffin didn't happen by accident. This was planned, but am I in danger? The truth is I just don't know. There might be a simple explanation for all this but right now I can't for the life of me work out what that is.

Why had their Alice used my name? She must have heard of me; otherwise it doesn't make sense. Had she been closely connected to me, in the past perhaps? Now that is a scary thought. These last years, I've had no interaction at all with anyone from my old life. Not even with the family or friends I left behind. Now I'm wondering if Tara has anything to do with this, or perhaps Max. Silly idea, why would they? What benefit is there in having me here?

There's nothing in Tara's demeanour to suggest she's being anything other than truthful. She's obsessed with looks and money, and why not? She's beautiful and knows it, whereas I'm plain and ordinary. Tara is tall, willowy and looks like a supermodel. All the clothes on her back are designer. I know because I've drooled over similar in the expensive shops in town. Everything about her is a world away from my own charity shop-bought outfit and cheap shoes.

Turning to me, Tara asks, 'You alright for time? You've come a long way, but you should have something to eat before you leave.'

I nod and check my mobile. My one and only friend, Ella, has texted me. She's asking how I've got on and when will I get back. I know Ella only too well; what she's really after is a night in some boozer getting legless. No way do I want any of that. I struggle to make ends meet as it is. I had to give up my own bedsit because I couldn't afford the rent. I was about to be thrown out when Ella came to my rescue. She lives in a grotty bedsit too, no bigger than my rabbit hole, but she kindly offered me her sofa and I owe her. But not today; I've got to see this through first.

The wake it is then, and hopefully I will get through it unscathed and unrecognised. I've worked hard these last three years at perfecting the art of invisibility – I'm the perfect blend-in package... a skill I'll certainly need for the next few hours.

The alternative doesn't bear thinking about. The vision of someone from my past standing there, finally taking their revenge, horrifies me.

THREE

I anticipated that Max and Tara would live in some style, they're the type, but I wasn't expecting this. As Max takes the car smoothly up the long drive, I stare open-mouthed at the sight in front of me. They live in a huge country house overlooking the River Bollin on the outskirts of Prestbury village. This is money country: top footballers' and other celebrities' favoured place to live.

The front of the house overlooks the narrow country lane we'd just driven along, then open fields, which appear to roll on for miles. No sign of the grimy city here. The front garden is spectacular. Bordering the drive are roses of every colour and hydrangea bushes in full bloom. Each shrub meticulously placed and kept in pristine condition.

Inside, the house is equally grand. As we walk along the hallway, I catch a glimpse inside each room we pass. Expensive furniture, lavish décor, the stuff of dreams. We stop outside the kitchen while Tara has a word with a group of people who I presume are the caterers. It's kitted out with what looks like every appliance known to man, including a huge range to cook on. I feel a pang of envy; this is so different from the one-ring gas job I usually cook on in Ella's bedsit.

'The wake is in the dining room.' She nods at a room at the end of the corridor. 'We'll join the others soon but first I'll sort your leg.'

As Max goes off to greet the guests, she leads the way into a large sitting room. It's a glorious space, and I wouldn't be surprised if it wasn't the most expensively furnished in the entire house. The centrepiece is a huge red velvet sofa covered in soft, squishy cushions. The sort you just want to dive onto and fall asleep.

My eyes are on stalks. I've never seen a house like this before never mind been inside one. 'This is beautiful,' I gasp. 'You're so lucky, it's like a palace.' I walk towards the French doors that lead from the sitting room into the back garden. Outside there's a sweeping lawn with flower borders, like in the front, each bed laid out in a matching pattern. A gardener's dream.

'We have a man to look after it,' Tara says with a smile. 'We couldn't tackle that lot on our own. Max doesn't have the time, and as far as I'm concerned, getting my hands muddy just doesn't appeal.' She wiggled her fingers at me. 'These nails cost a fortune to maintain. No way am I using them to dig around in the dirt.'

Not something I'd mind. Being able to grow things, especially my own vegetables, would suit me fine.

'Max must be very successful,' I say.

Tara gives me a smile of acknowledgement, but there's something else in her face, in the way she turns away and looks towards the door.

'Max doesn't like me discussing his work.'

Fair enough, I'll drop the topic but I can't help wondering why. Successful men are usually happy to have their achievements talked about.

Tara points to the lavish sofa and nods. 'Take a seat, I'll be back in a minute. Get rid of those tights too. I'm sure you don't want to be meeting the other guests like that.'

Tara is taking a risk telling me to sit on her gorgeous sofa. My leg could start bleeding again, and then I'd be mortified.

'This might sting a bit, but it will do the trick.'

The dab of cotton wool on my knee makes me wince; she wasn't wrong. Whatever she dabbed on my knee hurt like hell.

'There, that should fix it. We'd better go and meet the others. Max will be wondering where we've got to.'

This is the scary bit, the socialising with strangers. I'm no good with people I don't know. I daren't tell Tara; she won't understand. She's so confident and no doubt a brilliant hostess.

We head towards the dining room at the end of the corridor. I can hear people chatting, punctuated by the occasional peal of laughter. This is terrifying – strangers, questions and stares from people looking down their noses at me. I should have made an excuse and not come.

'Finally we can get a stiff drink,' Tara nudges. 'It's been a long, hard day. You must be hungry. There's plenty of food; it's buffet style so help yourself.'

In the centre of the dining room is a large table laden with food. All sorts of picky bits, as my friend Ella would say. But what I'm looking at is a long way from anything the two of us have ever eaten.

A smartly dressed waiter hands me a small plate and offers me a platter of what he tells me are canapés. I give him a fleeting smile and choose one: cream cheese and green olives. It looks so small that I take another, this time salmon with something I don't recognise on it. I'm way out of my comfort zone, this is so not me.

'We've not met.'

A huge man with swept-back blond hair and a suntan to die for towers above me. He's wearing an expensive suit, which must have been tailor-made for him the way it fits his larger-than-average frame.

'Nicco,' he tells me. 'And you are?'

'Donna.' One word, my name, and I'm stuck, any attempt at small talk has deserted me. There's an uncomfortable silence and then I say, 'I used to know Alice.' The words tumble from my mouth and sound like an admission of guilt. 'It was a long time ago,' I add hurriedly.

The man, Nicco, grins at me. 'I didn't know her well either. Alice was fixtures and fittings, always here but you rarely noticed her.'

I look around the room. 'She must have been popular, there's a lot of people here.'

'Max will have twisted a few arms. He was fond of Alice and wanted to give her a good send-off.'

I nod my head. 'He's certainly done that. The food, the drink and caterers to ensure no one goes hungry must be costing him a fortune.'

Words! I can hardly believe it, I'm almost having a conversation. I give Nicco a smile. He is actually easy to talk to. Despite his size, he isn't the least bit intimidating.

'Max can be a fool with his money. I know, I'm his accountant.' Nicco leans forward and whispers in my ear, 'But I guess Alice was special.'

'What exactly did she do?'

'Max runs his business from the house and Alice worked in the office here. She started out as a simple office assistant but soon became much more than that. She was Max's right arm; there was nothing about his little empire she didn't know.'

'It'll be hard to find someone else like her.'

'Impossible, I'd say.'

'Were you at the service?' I ask him.

'I missed it. I had an important meeting in Chester and got stuck on the motorway coming back.'

'Despite my good intentions, I missed it too.'

Ignoring my comment, Nicco says, 'Manchester, it's the twang, I'd know it anywhere. Whereabouts do you come from?'

'Longsight, close to the city centre.'

I've broken my own rule, I'm telling him things I shouldn't. Invisible, give nothing away, I remind myself, but it's too late, I've told him where I live.

'I know Manchester well. I've got a number of friends there, and two of my office staff live there as well.'

He knows people where I live. I have to end this conversation before I put my foot right in it.

'What do you do for a living?'

How do I answer that one? The night shift in a corner shop doesn't sound impressive at all. Not that I'm trying to impress him; all I really want is for him to leave me alone and find someone else to chat to. I've said too much already, broken all my own rules, down to nerves, I expect.

'Nothing much,' I shrug. 'I keep looking for something new, but you know how things are.'

'Like I say, I have contacts. I'll give you a couple of business cards, ring them and mention my name. Believe me, they'll snap you up.'

He can't know that, he's got no idea what my skill set is.

'That's kind of you but I don't want anything full time, not just yet.'

I don't want to explain that one either, to tell him that it's safer if I avoid strangers.

He reaches into his jacket and pulls out a number of business cards and sifts through them.

'I'll leave these with you. Don't forget what I said: when you decide you want a change, mention my name and any of these people will take you on without the fuss of having to apply.'

He pushes the cards into my hand. I can hardly refuse to

take them. He's trying to help and, who knows, one day I might be in a position to use them.

'Mine is in there, feel free to ring me if you've got any questions.'

'That's kind of you, thanks.' I genuinely mean that. This man, Nicco, could turn out to be a find.

'Can I get you a drink?' he asks.

My budget can only run to the odd can of lager; looking at the vast array of wines and spirits on the table, I'm lost.

'A small red wine, please,' I finally decide.

While he's gone, I take a look at the business cards, putting his in my jacket pocket. One of the others is for a software company, not for me, too much brain power needed. Another is for a wholesale company in Ancoats, a possible. But it's the last one that sends my head into a spin. It's for a company operating from an office in the city, one I'm very familiar with. For the second time today I'm looking at a name from my past.

FOUR

I meet a man at a wake, we get talking and he offers me work with my worst nightmare, the man I've spent the last three years keeping well away from. So why in leafy Cheshire does some stranger hand me the business card of someone I know, someone who lives miles away? Not without planning, that's for sure.

Nicco is back with the drinks. I take my wine and offer the business cards back to him.

'I'm sorry but none of these are any use to me.'

Did that sound convincing? Not to my ears, it didn't. My voice has gone all high pitched and I'm playing with my hair, giveaways for how anxious I feel... well, to me anyway.

'Keep them, you never know.' He gives me another smile. 'If you fancy working for any of those companies in the future, give me a ring,' he says.

I might look alright on the outside but my insides are shaking. I take a sip of wine hoping it'll calm my nerves. This man, Nicco, is a plant, has to be. I have to ask, not that I want to, but I can't leave things like this.

I wave the business card that is causing my pulse to race.

'I'm sure I've heard of him.' I'm trying to sound casual, as if my comment is just idle curiosity, but it's far from that.

Nicco takes the card off me.

'Sorry, I shouldn't have given you this one, the company no longer exists.'

That's a surprise.

'Fallen on hard times?' I ask.

'Andrew Wolfenden, the owner, is ill and the prognosis isn't good. He's relocated to his villa in the south of France.'

I'm not an unkind person, and it takes a lot to make me hate anyone, but Andrew Wolfenden is the exception. He was the man everyone I knew went to when they needed money, so I took the risk. Wolfenden told me not to worry, that he'd lend me whatever I wanted. I'm not a greedy person and borrowed only what was necessary. While I was earning, the repayments were not a problem. But my hours at the shop were reduced and there were many weeks when I couldn't pay the full amount. It was then I saw Andrew Wolfenden for what he is. He piled on the interest, and each week the threats got more real. I didn't understand how he could be like that. I had paid off the amount I'd borrowed but he said that didn't matter, that I still owed the interest. I was so afraid – I had to do something. He is the reason I changed my name and now live the life of a recluse. That may sound drastic but not when a man like Wolfenden is on your tail. I try not to hold grudges, and I'm sorry that he's ill, but it is poetic justice.

I have to know how much Nicco knows about the man. He is a link to my past and the way I've had to live since crossing paths with Wolfenden. Given the mystery surrounding today, I do wonder if meeting Nicco is coincidence or something more sinister.

'What sort of business was he in?'

I ask as if the question is simply me trying to make casual conversation.

'He was in finance,' Nicco says. 'That's what he told people, what he wanted them to believe. But the truth is Wolfenden was a money lender, one with a reputation for using dubious methods to make his customers pay up.'

'A right charmer then.' I force a smile.

'Charmer isn't really the word I'd use when describing Andrew. The truth is the man has all the charm of a Rottweiler on speed. At one time there was no reasoning with him. He decides to go after someone who owes him and he doesn't give up. These days he's a calmer person, the illness has done that, turned him into someone I can reason with.'

'You're an accountant, was he one of your clients?'

'For a while but I dropped him. When I dealt with him, Andrew was at his worst, volatile and intimidating. I can't have people like him coming to my offices.'

'Do you know who he sold his business to?'

This I can do with knowing. With luck they will find out that Alice is dead and drop the matter.

'Businesses owned by people like him don't get sold in the accepted way. It's rare that there is any legal stuff involved – no solicitors, for example. The customers are simply passed on to another lender for an agreed price.'

Nicco seems pleasant enough but all this talk about the man I have nightmares about is unnerving. That, plus the fact that, apart from the morsel on my plate, I've not eaten all day, makes me feel light-headed, so much so that I grab hold of Nicco's arm.

'Sorry but I feel a bit faint. It's warm in here,' I apologise.

'Why don't you sit down and I'll get you a tot of brandy and some food. I bet you've not eaten much today.'

I give him a small smile and nod. 'With the travelling to get here, I've not had much time to think of food.'

The truth is that I'm reeling from what Nicco has just told me. I can hardly believe it. I've got my life back. I'm finally free of the man I've been afraid of for so long. I'm not surprised I feel faint; it's such a weight off my mind.

Nicco returns with the food and brandy. I down the drink in one. I certainly need something stronger than wine; it's been a roller coaster of a day.

'Did you know Alice Anderson well?' he asks.

'Not really. We had a brief friendship then she moved on and that put an end to it.'

'She was an odd one, never spoke about her past or her family. She hated Tara with a passion. She told Max that his wife would ruin him if she got the chance.'

'Did she base that on anything in particular?'

'I've no idea... jealousy, I reckon. Mind you, she'd no chance with Max: Tara is his world.'

'Have you known them long?'

'I've known Max for a number of years and we still do the occasional bit of business together. Can I give you a word of advice? Avoid Tara at all costs. She's bad news.'

He's wrong about that, has to be. Tara has offered me nothing but kindness. Nicco is a mystery. He knows the man I'm desperate to forget and the woman who took my name. I trust my own instinct when it comes to liking people or not; if I had to choose, I'd go for Tara over Nicco any day of the week. But trying to work out why these people like each other or not isn't worth the brain power. I'll have left this place and these people behind within the hour.

I look over to where Tara is charming guests, topping up glasses and being a sparkling host. She notices me looking over and gives me a nod. I smile back, knowing that I won't be staying much longer and I'm unlikely to see any of this lot again.

How wrong I am.

FIVE

Tara spots me and Nicco chatting and comes across to join us.

'Nicco, how nice to see you,' she gushes. 'It's good of you to come, particularly as you didn't know Alice well.'

I don't know Tara but I can spot insincerity when I see and hear it. Nicco has just told me he doesn't like Tara, and I guess the feeling is mutual despite the show of affection.

'Max told me what happened. He seemed upset so I thought he could do with a little moral support,' Nicco replies.

Ignoring him, Tara turns and smiles at me.

'This is Donna, a friend of Alice. You two seem to have hit it off. I've been observing the pair of you,' she says, and I wonder why she's been watching me so closely.

'I've suggested a few firms that would be happy to take Donna on.'

Tara's face drops. 'Are you looking for work?' she asks me.

She said that with an edge to her voice. 'No, not really, but Nicco was kind enough to make a few suggestions in case I change my mind.'

Tara turned to Nicco again and, with a glacial stare, she

says, 'Max and I are about to make an offer of work to Donna ourselves.'

I'm not sure if she means that or is saying it to spite Nicco.

'We want the person who takes over from Alice to be someone who knew her, and you, Donna, are the obvious choice.'

Weird logic... What about experience and references, or even talking to me about it first?

'That's kind of you,' I tell her. 'But I'm not sure I'm up to it.'

'You can answer the phone, can't you? Organise Max's itinerary and handle the accounts.'

None of that sounds too hard, except the accounts, but it's a great offer.

'It's good of you to think of me, but even if I wanted to accept, you should know that I'm hopeless at figures. I would find the accounts part of the job tricky.'

I shouldn't have said that. What I should have done is waffle, blag my way into the job, but I can't. That wouldn't be honest and Tara would find out soon enough.

'We use a simple accounts package and Alice backed everything up on spreadsheets. She wrote instructions on how to use both. I'm sure you'll find it a piece of cake once you get going.'

She has a lot of faith in me. A woman who can barely add up in charge of the business accounts. But now she knows my weakness and has accepted it. I'd be a fool to turn the job down. And being here will give me time to work out who Alice was and who wanted me at her funeral.

'Thank you,' I say. 'But this has come out of the blue. I'd need time to think about it.'

'Max needs a new assistant fast. If you don't want the job, he will be on to the agency tomorrow, and they will fix him up within hours.'

I feel like she's making it difficult to say no, but why Tara is so keen for me to take it is a mystery. I know I have no choice but to accept, it's the only way I'll find out who Alice Anderson really is, and who invited me to the funeral.

'I'd love to accept your offer.' There, I've said it. For better or worse I am going to be working for the pair. I just hope I've made the right decision.

'Max will be thrilled. He's been worried sick about who would take over. I know Alice would be pleased, and you'll fit in just fine.'

I'm not sure about that but I say nothing.

'You don't mind if I steal Donna from you?' She takes my arm and turns from Nicco.

'Of course not.' He gives me a wink. 'Good luck, I hope you're happy here.'

'I'll take you for a quick look around the house and the office where you will be working. Alice lived here in the annexe, it was more convenient all round. Max often needs things at short notice, and Alice was happy to work all hours. We thought it only fair to offer her accommodation here. We'd like it if you did the same.'

Lucky Alice. Living here, closeted away, not seeing anyone from outside, must have suited her. It strikes me that I'd be happy with that arrangement too.

'Your home is fantastic and huge.' I smile at Tara.

'Nothing to do with me, the design and size is all down to Max. There are eight bedrooms and an annexe, would you believe. There are only three of us. Max and me, plus our daughter Hanna. The reality is the house is an indulgence on Max's part. We could house a small army in a place this size.'

What interests me more is the daughter, Hanna. Was she at the funeral? If she had attended, she didn't return home with us. Leaving that for now, I ask, 'How did Alice die?'

Tara is silent for a moment as if considering how to reply. Max had the same problem as I remember.

'A tragic accident,' she says at last. 'It's all still a bit raw... D'you mind if we don't talk about it right now.'

She sniffs and runs shaky fingers over her cheeks. It really is raw if this is how talking about it affects her. A change of subject is needed.

'Are you sure I will be able to fill Alice's shoes? Like I told you, I don't have much experience in office work. A computer training course the job centre sent me on is about it. But I was good, I passed with top marks. During the course, I did work experience at the local council offices too. I enjoyed the job, but they didn't keep me on. Perhaps my face didn't fit.'

'I doubt that. It'll have been down to them having to operate within a tight budget.' She nods at me. 'You and Alice are so alike. When she was first offered the job, she had her doubts too. But she was a natural and within a few weeks was thoroughly enjoying the work. She picked up things quick and was a godsend to Max. He often has to travel or see clients at short notice. She organised the meetings and accommodation. Alice was a whiz with the accounts too. Max does have an accountant but likes to keep an eye on all things financial himself. He trusted Alice absolutely and was very grateful to her, which is why he was only too happy to organise the funeral and pay for it. She had no family so there was no one else to offer.'

'That's very kind of him. I'm sure Alice would be grateful.'

'She'd be pleased too that we've found someone who knew her to take her place. Excellent in the office she might have been, but Alice did not like strangers. That's why I thought it so odd when you turned up today.'

Tara has offered me the job but her tone suggests that she isn't sure. It seems the other Alice was a lot like me – wary of people she didn't know – and now Tara is unsure if she can trust me or not.

'I had to come.' I smile. 'We might not have seen each other in ages but I did like Alice.'

Tara nods and her expression lightens. She seems satisfied for now. But can I do Alice's job? Talking business, working with figures is not something I'll feel confident with. On the plus side, a job here would help me get answers to the questions burning a hole in my brain, and that makes the prospect more appealing.

'What type of business is Max involved in?'

'He's a property developer. Basically he buys land and builds on it. But he chooses land in desirable areas and the houses are huge, palatial in some instances.'

Now I understand where the money for this enormous house comes from.

'Max has an office in the city but these days he mostly works from home. The traffic, the hold-ups driving in got to him, so working here is a good solution.'

'Clearly he's successful in what he does,' I say, looking around the beautifully decorated room we're standing in.

Too much? Tara doesn't think so if the superior look on her face is anything to go by. But I am genuinely interested. I'm curious about people who make money. Not that I have any chance of emulating them, I'll never have the start-up cash, but perhaps I can learn a lesson or two.

'Max built the business from scratch and deserves the success. The business is exceptionally profitable; even so, he isn't a man to stay still. He's ambitious, takes risks and doesn't put limits on what's possible. Hence the moods and the short temper. He's a shrewd operator, he knows the market and he is adept at buying in the right area, like around here.' She smiles. 'This house is one of his. It was his special project, and the money spent over the top, but it's a great family home and we love it.'

She'd be stupid not to, the house is a dream and way beyond what most people can even hope for. We're back in the sitting room. The pair of us stand and stare out of the French doors at the garden, me thinking how gorgeous it is; as for Tara, I can't read her.

Had Alice liked it here? She must have done, living in a place like this is everyone's dream, and I bet it was the same for Alice but for different reasons. Life in a small village, working and living under the same roof, not having to mix too much with the outside world. Just what a woman with a stolen name would want... and I'm the expert.

I stare at the beautiful back garden; it's perfect in every way. It must be wonderful to live in such surroundings, so quiet and peaceful. Where I live there's the continual roar of traffic, people arguing in the streets and violent behaviour from others living in the same building as me. I'm envious of this family. I can't help it. I'm not a jealous person but this is something else.

But I mustn't forget the real reason I'm here today. Fate has dealt me a lucky hand. This job is my ticket to unravelling the mystery of Alice.

I need a plan, to learn my lines and not get them wrong. Alice did not take my name by accident. She may not have come to work here by accident either. An interesting thought and one that gets me thinking.

'You have a daughter; was she at the funeral?'

I want to meet her; she could be useful.

'Hanna refused to come to the service.' Tara folds her arms and shakes her head. 'She's twenty-three, but at times she can behave like a petulant teenager. That she wasn't there is embarrassing, people notice and whisper. She got on well with Alice, for which we are grateful. Alice encouraged her, teased out the things she was good at. Hanna is hankering after starting her own business, a coffee shop in the neighbouring village. Both Alice and I were behind her and would have helped. But Hanna wanted to go it alone, silly of her because she needs money, and Max is key to her getting what she wants.'

I don't comment, I haven't met the girl. I'm still looking out at the garden. At the bottom, on the left of the beautifully tended lawn, is a rough patch of ground. On it is a large enclosure and what looks like a huge shed. I'm about to ask but Tara gets in first.

'That's Max's preserve. Don't ask me why but he's obsessed with pigs; he always has been. As far as I'm concerned, they're horrible creatures, dirty and destructive with their rooting about on the land. Max doesn't think so, they're his pride and joy. If he has any spare time, he spends it over there. If ever we can't find him, that's where he'll be. Hanna helps him but only if forced; she's no pig lover either. She likes animals, sweet little things, puppies, kittens and the like, but Max won't have them in the house. Pigs are his thing and nothing else. We hadn't lived here a week when Max moved the bloody things in. That man has strange tastes.'

I'm with Tara, strange tastes indeed, and pigs aren't my favourite creatures either. Having met the man in his expensive designer suit, I think it an odd hobby for Max; I can't imagine him mucking out pigs, somehow. As our conversation comes to an end, I know this is my shot to find out why I'm here.

'I was invited here today, by email, it was unsigned. I presume it must have been sent to me by a member of the family. What I don't understand is how did you get my email address?'

I want an answer to this one. I've lived the life of a near hermit these last three years. No one from my old life knows how to find me. No one knows about the name Donna Slade either. I don't know what I expected but Tara doesn't look in the least fazed by the question.

'Hanna sent out the invites, so Alice must have given her your details.'

That can't be true. This Alice or whoever she was can't have had any idea where I was or my email address. Or am I wrong? Was the invite, and the job offer, part of something else, a scheme to lure me here? Nicco knows the man I owe money to, and that man is unforgiving. I'm afraid that I have walked into a trap. Otherwise, how can Hanna, a girl I've never set eyes on, find out so much about me?

SIX

I can't believe what Tara just told me, and I now have even more questions spinning around my head. How much does this Hanna know about me? Has she discussed me with Tara or Max? If she has, things could get tricky. Tara's face gives nothing away. I need her to say something, anything that would explain things. I want to know what's going on here. That little voice in my head is telling me to leave. Get the hell out of here while I still can.

'You must tell me about Alice,' Tara says. 'How did you meet her?'

My heart sinks at the question. It's the same one I want to ask her, but not yet. I need Tara to trust me. Whatever I tell her has to sound believable, not something I'm good at. Telling blatant lies makes me nervous.

'We met in an estate agent's.' I smile. 'I was struggling to find a flat to rent in my price range, and she put me in touch with a landlord who could help.' *Be careful*, I tell myself, or you'll trip yourself up. 'After that we stayed friends for a while, went out for the odd drink, but when she moved away, we lost touch.'

'That's exactly like Alice to help you like that.' Tara smiles. 'She was always sorting things for Max. Putting right his mistakes and covering for him when he was late for meetings. I'm pleased you will be taking over from her. The job comes with a generous wage and rooms of your own if you choose to live in. We're some distance from Manchester and the commute would be difficult if you have to travel by bus.'

She's right, look at today, I was late for the funeral. Both living and working here will be more than just convenient, I'll have proper accommodation, safe, warm and noise-free. It is the perfect opportunity to dig deep and try to get to the bottom of the Alice conundrum.

'Are you sure Max will be okay with this?'

'Oh, don't worry about that. You're just the kind of girl Max is looking for.'

An odd thing to say when Tara has known me all of two hours. Would she be so keen to employ me if she knew I'm a fraud, that since I met her and Max, I've been lying through my eyeteeth. I must take extra care with what I tell them, I can't afford to slip up. Stick to the story, keep any talk of my past simple and I should be okay.

There is one thing that bothers me, and that's all the official stuff needed to employ me. It's all in my proper name, Alice Anderson. Using the name Donna Slade hasn't been a problem up to now. I've worked for some shady people and only got away with it because the jobs have been cash in hand with no questions asked. My only option now is to bluff my way through. I've no idea how, but I'll have to think of something.

'I'll show you round,' Tara tells me. 'We'll look at the annexe first; that'll be your own space. Feel free to bring your stuff and settle in whenever you like.'

'Later?' I ask. 'When do you want me to start work?'

'Max will want you in the office as soon as possible. He's

always super busy, works day and night, and needs all the help he can get.'

I have important things to sort out myself before moving is even possible. First is telling Ella; me leaving will hit her hard as she relies on what little rent I give her. I feel guilty about that; she did give me somewhere to stay when I had nowhere else. But I can't turn my back on what I've been offered; hopefully Ella will see that too and forgive me.

Tara leads me from the sitting room and along a hallway. There are rooms off each side and a seating area at the end with a sofa looking out at another fabulous view of the front garden.

We walk up the elegant staircase and are on another corridor. Tara opens the first door on the right.

'This will be your space. At one time it was a huge bedroom. Max had it converted into three smaller rooms – a sitting room, bedroom and bathroom. It's large enough for one, and there's plenty of cupboard space for your things.'

I walk inside and nearly faint. Large is an understatement. It's practically a small flat. There is a lounge, a double bedroom and a bathroom, all furnished with what looks like new stuff.

'All this for me?' I gasp in disbelief.

Ignoring me, she continues. 'You have your television and music system over there.' She points. 'There's a laptop on the desk in the corner. If there's anything else you want, just ask.'

Anything else, unlikely. Have I fallen asleep and landed in some alternate universe? This is a world away from Ella's bedsit and anywhere else I've lived. It's just perfect.

'This is amazing. I can't believe how big this place is.'

'I am sure Alice would be delighted to see you so happy. She was a wonderful woman who wanted only to help people where she could. It's bound to take you a little while to settle in. Max will show you the office when you're ready and go over what he wants you to do. He's got a couple of important meetings later this month and will need some paperwork completing before then.'

I nod. 'Of course, I'll be only too happy.'

At that moment the front doorbell rings, interrupting us.

'I bet that's someone who missed the wake,' Tara says. 'I'll sort it out, then we'll have a chat.'

Left on my own I look around my new surroundings. I run my hand over the furniture with what I'm sure is a silly smile on my face. Going to the funeral had been a godsend after all. Look where I've ended up.

'I hope you like it here.'

I spin round to see a young woman staring at me from the doorway. She's tall and, as my aunt would say, big-boned. She has long, mousey hair and a pale complexion, so pale it's debatable whether she's seen the light of day in weeks. Her bright-blue eyes are startling, the colour of a summer sky. And I can tell they're sharp; I bet they don't miss a trick. Just like her father. This, I take it, is Hanna.

'Your mum and dad are kind people.'

There's a pause as her gaze drifts towards a painting of wildflowers on the wall.

'This was Alice's place. I heard Mum has offered you her job, so I suppose it's yours now.'

Hanna speaks to me as if I've broken some unwritten rule in occupying these rooms. Finished looking at the picture, she pushes past me and plonks herself on the sofa.

'I used to come in here and chat to her at night. We'd sit here and talk for hours. She was a good listener and she understood how things are. If she'd lived, Alice would have helped me.'

I presume she's talking about the café she wants to open but I'm not going to ask; I've too much on my mind as it is.

'I miss her.'

The smile has disappeared from her face. She's upset; I'd

like to help, but I don't feel able. I didn't know Alice and I don't know Hanna, so it's likely I'd just make things worse. But I've got to say something.

'I'm not Alice but I hope we can be friends too.' The girl's blue eyes meet mine and I see a flicker of doubt. She doesn't trust me, but why should she? I'm a stranger.

She's back on her feet, making for the door.

'Sorry, I didn't mean to embarrass you. It's being in this room again, knowing someone else will be calling it their own and doing Alice's job. Alice was the only friend I had. I thought I was her only friend too, but today you showed up.'

What does she mean by that? She's young and free and has just told me her father's deceased admin assistant was her only friend. It has to be a lie; a young woman like Hanna must have a large circle of friends. Until I know her better, I'll watch what I say; my life these last three years is off limits.

Hanna wipes tears from her cheeks. Looking at her, I can't see either Tara or Max in her features. She's Tara's daughter but has none of her beauty. Tara has fine features and beautiful blonde hair. Hanna must think this grossly unfair, considering how her hair is tied up in a ponytail, but still small tufts stick out all over.

'If you're serious about taking the job, I want to know that you're not going to run out on us. I want us to be friends... Please promise me you'll stay.'

Those bright eyes cloud over as she speaks, and I see her lips quiver. This unexpected reliance on me is uncomfortable.

'Why would I leave? This is an amazing opportunity,' I assure her. 'Tara has offered me nothing but kindness, not to mention a job and somewhere to live. I'd be a fool to give that up.'

'You think that now but there will come a day when you'll regret being here. You might like her now but take my word for it, Tara is not an easy woman to get along with.'

She's her daughter, there's bound to be fireworks every so often. I'm sure I'll get on with Tara just fine. Max too; he'd been quick to help me at the funeral and he stood up for me against those women. I don't know the girl but wonder if Hanna is lying, trying to put me off. Whether she's telling the truth or not, I want this job. In the unlikely event Tara does turn out to be a pain, I'll just have to grit my teeth and deal with it. I decide to park what she's told me and wait on events. Foolish or wise, I've no idea. All I know is that I've got a job, accommodation, so for the time being I'm sorted.

'She's not that bad, surely.' I smile at her.

'You'll have to make up your own mind. I daren't say any more,' she says, looking worryingly at the door, as if someone might be outside listening.

What a strange thing to say. Why does Hanna think she can't say what she wants in her own home?

Her words plant a niggle in my head.

'If Alice liked you, then I'm sure I will too,' Hanna says. 'Don't take any notice of me today. Alice's passing hit me hard, and seeing you here, all new and fresh and about to take her place, upset me.'

Time for a change of subject. The girl looks close to tears.

'It's a bit isolated here. Do you get out much?'

'I know what you're doing,' is her immediate reply. 'You think talking about something else will take my mind off Alice. I will get over losing her, but it'll take time. I valued our friendship. Now she's gone I have no one to confide in. My parents don't have time for me. I'm nothing but an afterthought in their lives.'

Hanna must be wrong; she's an only daughter, and I'm sure her parents dote on her.

'Can I ask you something, Hanna?'

The girl shrugs. 'I can't promise I'll know the answer or want to tell you if I do.'

An attitude I'm not keen on. Hanna is shaping up to be someone who likes to hold the balance of power in a situation.

'Your mum told me that it was you who invited me to the funeral. How did you get hold of my email address?'

'Tara's wrong, it had nothing to do with me.'

With that she leaves me to puzzle over what she'd said. Alice couldn't have known how to contact me. That would only be possible if she knew about my new life. So how had the sender, whoever they are, found out my email address? And if Alice genuinely didn't know my email, then she couldn't have told a member of this family. That can only mean one thing: someone is on to me. Someone knows my name and, for reasons of their own, wanted me at the funeral.

If I'm right about the email, the protection a different identity gave me has just gone up in smoke.

SEVEN

In the last few hours, I've attended a funeral for a woman who was masquerading as me, met two of the Cheshire rich set, and been offered a job and a place to live. All in all, not a bad outcome.

So why the feeling that something's not right?

What Hanna said has got to me, made me nervous. She said nothing that should upset me. Who am I kidding? The email has rattled me. My sensible head says Alice must have given her my email address and Hanna is lying. But why? What does she know? And what is she going to do with the information?

I hope Hanna doesn't turn out to be a liability. For all I know she might be a habitual liar, someone who'll spy on me and gossip about things I'd prefer kept secret. On the other hand, win her friendship and Hanna could be of value. She spent time with Alice and is probably the one who knew her best. I'll use that, make Hanna my friend and see where it gets me.

There's a knock on the door: Tara's back.

'Sorry, I got waylaid downstairs. It seems a pity to wait until tomorrow, would you like to see the offices now?' she asks with a smile.

The scary bit. The work I'll be expected to do here is about to become real.

'Max is having a lie down before dinner. It has been a heavy day for the both of us; Alice's death has hit him hard. Drowning his sorrows in several glasses of whisky at the wake has done him no good at all. I did get a chance to tell him about you accepting the job though and like me he thinks it a great idea. He wants to know if you can start tomorrow.'

Sooner than I'd thought but no biggie. I'll collect my stuff from Ella's later. 'Tomorrow's fine,' I reply.

'In that case I'll show you where you'll be working.'

I follow her along the corridor. She opens a door and gestures for me to enter.

'This is the office Alice worked from and now it's yours,' she says. 'It's got everything you should need. If there's anything else, just shout.'

It looks well laid out but my experience of working in an office is limited. There's a large desk in the centre of the room with a computer on it. That interests me more than anything else. Like the laptop in my rooms there could be something on there to help me find answers, information about Alice, for instance. I'll go through everything with a fine-tooth comb in the hope that I strike lucky. Beside it is a unit with a printer. To hand is a telephone, and against the wall, several filing cabinets and shelves. The entire setup is professional but a little frightening. There's also a door leading to the adjoining office. I presume that's Max's domain.

Tara nods as if reading my thoughts.

'That door is kept locked at all times,' she says firmly. 'Under no circumstances are you to enter that room.'

Her voice has an edge to it and her features have hardened, confirmation that Max's office is very much off-limits.

'If I'm to replace Alice and one day perhaps be his PA., it makes little sense to me if I'm banned from his office.' The words are out of my mouth before I can censor them. Tara gives me a look that says I'm out of line.

'That's the way it has to be,' she snaps at me. 'You need to know nothing else other than Max hates to be disturbed when he's working.'

A feeble excuse and one I don't believe. My *something is odd* antenna is at it again.

'Interruptions are guaranteed to anger him. Any problems, come to me first,' she instructs.

Separate work areas, so no opportunity to ask him questions. Had it been like this with Alice? Until now, I haven't given much thought to the nuts and bolts of the job, but now I have even more questions. But first things first. 'What will the bulk of my duties consist of?'

'You'll have documents to key in, emails to send, which Max will give you, and you'll keep an eye on the accounts. But don't worry, it's all written down on one of Alice's famous spreadsheets. I can assure you the days will be varied,' she says. 'You needn't worry about getting bored.'

That was all well and good, but something tells me I could easily put my foot in it. This thing about Max's privacy is a touchy area.

'Is there any reason why Max needs to work alone?' More words that fall out of my mouth. Well, I have to ask. This setup is ludicrous. In an office environment with phone calls and emails coming in, I will need to speak to him. 'What happens if something urgent comes up?'

'You find me,' her sharp reply. 'If I'm out, you ring my mobile and I'll deal with whatever it is. It's not difficult, Donna; you'll soon get used to how things have to be.'

This is the first time she's spoken to me in that tone since I met her, and I don't understand the problem. For a moment there, Tara's mask slipped. Pandering to Max, ensuring that what he wants he gets, must wear her out, mentally as well as physically. The Tara I've seen today is the glossed-up version, a woman playing a part. This palaver about working alone suggests that Max has secrets. I make a mental note to prise more information about this setup from Hanna when I see her next.

'Familiarise yourself with the office, then take a proper look at your rooms. Dinner is at seven. If you're going to be living with us, we'd love to get to know you. Please eat with us tonight. It would mean a lot to both of us. Please say you can stay. We'll arrange transport for you to go back to your place and organise things afterwards.'

She's staring at me, waiting for me to agree. The problem is I have plans. I need to pick up my stuff from Ella's. I don't have so much as a toothbrush with me.

'Do not let me down, I won't appreciate it.'

The tone of her voice is harsh; the lovely Tara is running out of patience while the nice Tara appears to have taken time off. She checks the clock on the office wall and decides it's time to leave.

'You felt unwell at the wake; a friend told me you almost fainted.'

'It was the heat and I hadn't eaten much. Nicco got me a tot of brandy and I was fine.'

I don't miss the fact that her eyes blaze at me when I mention Nicco's name.

'Dinner is not for several hours yet; if you're hungry in the meantime, help yourself to what you want from the fridge.'

As my stomach rumbles, I think to myself that I might just take her up on that offer. Tara wants me to have dinner with the three of them, that will need some working out. I must get my stuff from the bedsit, which means a bus ride there and back. It's five already so it'll be pushing it.

Tara nods at me from the doorway and is gone. She's got stuff on her mind, how to make me toe the line more than likely. The reality is I should be grateful for my lot. I wouldn't get this chance anywhere else. Moody or not, Tara has done me an immense favour today and I won't forget it.

No sooner has she disappeared than Hanna is at the office door. 'Got a fag?' she asks.

I shake my head. 'I don't smoke.'

'If you go out, will you buy me some?'

'I will if you give me the money.'

'I've got nothing, can't you lend me some?'

'All I've got in the world is some loose change, Hanna. Have you considered giving it up? I look at her and smile. 'Hard work, I know, and not pleasant. Have you tried patches?'

She stares back at me as if I'm from another planet. 'I've got no intention of giving it up. I smoke because it helps and not just tobacco either.'

She gives me a knowing look and I understand only too well what she means. I've been down that road myself. Drugs are insidious and sold to girls like Hanna only too easily.

'You think you've been hired to replace Alice but you're wrong,' she jibes at me. 'Soon Tara will ask you to keep an eye on me and other things you won't like.'

'I'm sure you've got that wrong.'

'No, I haven't. My mother puts on a good show. She's an expert liar; she has to be. A word of advice: think carefully before you believe anything she says to you.'

This is sour grapes because I can't buy her cigarettes. 'I'm here to work in the office, that's it. I won't spy on you, Hanna, and I won't tell tales to your parents, I promise.'

'Good, speak to them about me and you'll regret it. Right now, I like you but don't make me change my mind. I'm not someone you should cross; I don't want you to come to any harm.'

'Is that a threat?' She's got no idea. 'I'll warn you once: I'm not someone you should take on. If you knew my history, you wouldn't even think what you just said to me never mind speak it.'

My first impression of Hanna is that she's friendly enough when it suits her. When it doesn't, she's a different girl. There could be lots of reasons why she resorts to threats, although right now I can't think of any. She's grown up in a secure home with good parents; she should count herself lucky. It's possible that jealousy is at the bottom of it, that living in her mother's shadow has made her resentful. If I could help her I would, but that's probably a thankless task. It's becoming evident that she has a complex personality, and, besides, my time is needed elsewhere.

'I hope you can stick up for yourself,' she warns.

I've no idea what's going on in that head of hers: threats, warnings... I don't believe a word of it.

'Alice had the guts to stand her ground. Things can get tough working for Max and Tara. She's demanding, expects people to do as they're told without question. She'll grind you down, Donna. You need to be one tough cookie to work for either of them. My problem is that in spite of what you say, you don't look that tough to me.'

She's wrong. She just doesn't know it yet.

Hanna's face breaks into a grin. She looks my skinny frame up and down while shaking her head. I'm well aware that there's hardly anything of me, the life I've led has done that.

'You're too thin to be a threat to anyone. I reckon you're a wimp. First sign of trouble and you'll bail.'

'Don't worry about me, Hanna. You'd be wise not to under-estimate what I'm capable of. I'm more than able to fight my corner and win.'

I can't tell from her face whether she believes me or not, but she should. My life these last years has been hard; I wouldn't have made it through if I hadn't learned how to stick up for myself.

This little chat has proved useful. She's shown me another side of her personality, one I don't like much. Friend or foe? I'd prefer it to be friend. Then she turns everything she's told me on its head.

'I don't mean to be a pain. I get carried away at times... think everyone is against me. I want to like you, I really do, but I find relationships hard, even with my parents. I hope Max and Tara give you an easy time. I want you to stay. I need someone I can talk to. You will talk to me, won't you, Donna?'

I nod in response. 'Of course I will, Hanna, I want us to be friends too.'

The bravado has gone, as is her criticism of me. Having said her piece, she walks off along the corridor and disappears down the stairs. I'm left trying to work out why she'd want to tell me all that stuff about Tara. She meant every word and that bothers me.

EIGHT

The following morning, I wake up feeling dreadful. Someone's clashing cymbals together in my head; well, that's what it feels like. It's my first day in a new job; I'm eager to make a good impression but my brain won't join in.

It's all my own fault so no good putting the blame on anyone else. When I left the house last night, my intentions were good: I needed my stuff, and decided to pick it up and get back in time for dinner with the family.

But that's not how it worked out.

I made the mistake of waiting at the bedsit for Ella to turn up so I could say goodbye. I had to, no way could I disappear from her life and say nothing. She'd been a friend when I needed one, and I'll always be grateful for that.

As much as I like her, Ella has a wild streak and has never learned to tame it. She's out every night, takes drinks from anyone who offers then stumbles back to her bedsit well after midnight.

The poor girl was in tears when I told her my news. She said I'm the only friend she can trust and begged me not to go. I explained about my new job and the fabulous house I'll live in, but that upset her even more. She clung to me, tears running down her cheeks. I felt so guilty that when she asked me to have one last drink with her, I agreed. I didn't see any harm in it. What harm could one drink do?

We got comfy on Ella's sofa, and I went over again what had happened after the funeral. We chatted, laughed and Ella kept filling up our glasses. Neither of us realised just how much wine we'd drunk. And not only wine, we'd finished each glass with a shot of vodka. Feeling the worse for wear and realising it was now the small hours, I had no choice but to sleep on her sofa again.

* * *

The next morning, the bus ride back to the house is a killer. I've already had two coffees and a bunch of painkillers, but as I stare down at my sports bag stuffed with my belongings, the noise of the engine makes my head pound and my bones ache. Thankfully I don't have to sleep on that lumpy sofa ever again. I've no idea how far the house is from Longsight, but the bus journey is long and boring. I take a swig from the bottle of water I'd packed and pray I'll look and feel better before Tara sees me.

The bus stops in the village centre. Slinging the sports bag over my shoulder, I walk the rest of the way. I'm hoping I can sneak up to my rooms and have a wash before any of the family sees me.

My heart races as I open the door with my new key to find Tara standing in the hallway with a frown on her face and arms folded.

'You didn't make dinner last night.'

Now I feel as if I've broken another unwritten rule.

'Max was disappointed and so was I. We don't appreciate being let down, particularly as we have given you so much.'

That's me told; she's regretting her generosity already. Do I feel guilty about missing dinner? I did, but not now. I want to ask her what makes her think she can dictate what I do outside working hours. But I bite my tongue. I already know that telling her my friend needed me won't make a difference to her mood, so I mentally chalk it up: in future, if asked to dine with the family, make sure I don't let them down.

'I hope you've got a good excuse, Donna. You'll need one.'

Why? I look at her with glazed eyes. What to say? I feel like a naughty child and the look on her face doesn't help. It's a sort of mix of worry and anger. Is explaining my absence even worth it? Probably not but I have to tell her something. No mention of all the cheap white wine I drank; in the mood she's in, that won't go down well at all.

'Sorry, Tara, I went back to the bedsit to get my stuff. I was done in after the day I'd had. I didn't mean to miss dinner, but I fell asleep in a friend's bedroom. I'm afraid I couldn't help myself. I doubt I'd have been much company anyway.'

There's a flicker of a smile on her lips but it comes to nothing. She's still not happy.

'I don't like it when people ignore my invitations, and I particularly wanted you to join us for dinner last night. It was meant to be your first night with us.'

She's piling it on, making me feel as guilty as sin. I hope this isn't the norm or I'll have no life at all outside this house.

'Remember that in future. It's for your own good, Donna. You live here therefore you come to meals if invited. The only reason you'll be excused is if you're ill or away on business for Max.'

For my own good. What does she mean by that? Forget it, Donna, it's just words, I tell myself. I won't remember what she said anyway, my head's still banging after last night. It'll be a miracle if I get through the day.

'Max wants to see you straight away.'

Her voice wavers as she says Max's name and her hands are shaking. 'Are you okay?' I ask in good faith. Seconds later, I wish I'd kept my mouth shut. Tara gives me a filthy look, takes the heavy gym bag with all my belongings in it and tosses it into a corner. I wince; the bag contains one or two glass ornaments that had once belonged to my aunt Nancy, the one person in my life I was actually fond of. A little of my old life I've kept with me through thick and thin. I don't want what I have left of my aunt smashed to pieces. I'm about to voice my objection but one look at Tara's expression and I change my mind. Her face is hard and angry. Something I can put up with? If I want answers to the mystery of Alice, I'll have to.

'From now on you must behave, Donna. I don't want to have to reprimand you again.'

Reprimand... What does she think I am, some sort of servant?

She nods at my bag. 'You can sort that later.'

I watch her hurry off up the stairs and disappear into Max's office. I'd like to try and help her, but a woman like Tara will never let me get that close. The way she just behaved you'd think missing dinner last night was the sin of sins. If that telling-off is the norm, I'm in for a bumpy ride.

'Not what you expected,' a voice says from behind me. 'And it'll get worse. She can't help it. Tara is under a lot of stress, and she can't cope. One of these days she'll crack.'

Why is she stressed? I wonder. Is it the business? I would imagine that Max looks after that. Perhaps the pair have marriage problems. Whatever is wrong, Tara is suffering.

'Has something happened to upset her?' I ask.

Hanna grins at me, folds her arms, and nods. 'Something upsets her most days. Yesterday at dinner it was about Max and what he's done. She aired his faults in front of both me and Maria. Screamed at Max, she did, then smacked him one across the face. She didn't win though; he threw the words right back at her. She needs to be careful; she'll cross him once too often.'

Hanna's exaggerating; it'll have been a simple argument between husband and wife. All couples have them, I imagine. I could probe further but decide it's not worth it.

'Don't you want to know what the argument was about?'

Not getting involved is all very well but, whether I want to know or not, Hanna is determined to tell me.

'Tara pretended it was about the way Maria had cooked dinner, but it wasn't. It was about the usual.'

I've no idea what *the usual* is so can't comment.

'It's a shame you weren't here, you missed a treat. I hope whatever you were up to was worth it.'

She's looking at me with those piercing blue eyes of hers. For a moment I feel as if she can see right through me, spot a lie from a hundred paces. Even so, there's no way I'm telling her where I was or who with. Life in that bedsit and my friend Ella is my business. All talk about my whereabouts last night needs closing down.

'I was in my room. I'd had a heavy day, what with the funeral and the long bus ride. I fell asleep and didn't wake until this morning. That's why I missed the meal.'

She nods at the sports bag.

'That's a lie. I saw you come through the front door before Tara's ear-bashing with that bag in your hand.'

Observant of her, but this topic is going no further, so I change the subject. 'Are your mum and dad talking to each other this morning?'

'Not really. Tara is being careful what she says, and at breakfast Max hid behind the newspaper.'

'Come on then, tell me, what is the *usual*?'

'She never actually accuses Max, says what's needed; instead she rants about something unconnected. Last night she thought the lamb was overdone and gave Maria hell about it. Maria ran back to the kitchen crying. Tara went after her, but Maria wasn't having any of it and went home. That annoyed both me and Max; he insisted Tara ring and apologise. Tara refused and got the blame for ruining dinner.'

Good job I missed it. Witnessing Tara behave like that would have embarrassed me no end. The picture I have of her in my head is quite different. Beautiful, witty and kind... Mind you, that opinion is rapidly changing, and not because of what Hanna is telling me, but from my own experience.

'You still haven't told me.'

'Max is having an affair.

Now that does surprise me. This seemingly perfect marriage is blighted by his other woman.

'Her name is Isabel and he's been seeing her for months. Tara knows her, and at one time they used to be friends. But she's never been to the house.' My head spins as I recognise the name – Isabel was that awful woman at the funeral, the one who judged me, and who Max rescued me from. He's having an affair with her?

'Do you know her?' Donna asked.

'I've seen her, but we've never spoken. Tara needs to get that pretty head of hers out of the sand and give him hell. No woman should stand for what she does. They are a nightmare to live with, Donna, you have no idea. All I want to do is leave here and them far behind.'

I wasn't lucky enough to have two parents. I had a mother, not that she deserves the title, and an absent father. My mother and I lived with a variety of relatives, and I was rarely happy. The exception was when we stayed with my aunt Nancy. She liked me and I liked her. As a child I used to wish with all my heart that she was my mother. Hanna has no idea how lucky she is.

I'm saying no more. I'm not sure if I can trust Hanna, and if

Max finds out I've been gossiping, he won't like it. I'm not simply working here to please Max and Tara, I have an agenda of my own and would prefer a calm environment. With luck I'll be in and out of this place in no time. Max having an affair doesn't concern me.

'When it first started, Tara asked him straight about it, but Max blew his top,' Hanna tells me whether I want to know or not. 'Tara got upset, screamed and shouted then retired to her bed for the rest of the day. She soon realised making a scene about the mistress isn't worth the aggro, so the bouts of temper are always about something else, like the lamb last night. He's a crap husband and father, Donna. He doesn't give a damn about me or Tara. In the world of Max, we don't matter.'

I don't believe that for a moment. The Max that I met yesterday was kind and caring, he rescued me from Isabel, and he seemed in awe of his wife. Plus, who hates their own child anyway? I'm sure Hanna has got it wrong.

'Do you and Tara talk about Isabel?'

'It's never mentioned. Despite the temper, Tara hankers after a quiet life with no hassle, but that's impossible living with Max. If either of us faces up to him, criticise his behaviour, we suffer for it.'

I'm having difficulty believing Max is so selfish. If Hanna is telling the truth, from my own experience with Tara she'd have thrown him out by now, surely? And why confide in me? I've no idea what she expects me to do.

Time to lift the mood, drop all talk of her parents, switch it to something she likes. 'Your mum tells me you have ambitions to build a business, a coffee shop.'

The switch worked, there's an instant change in Hanna's mood, her face lightens, and I actually get a smile.

'I plan to open it in a village about five miles away. There's a number of empty shops next to the canal, a perfect spot, and the start-up rent is cheap. Even so, my big problem is the money.

Max promised to fund the initial costs. I've asked him several times, but he always fobs me off. I've decided to give him until the end of this month, then I'll go to the bank for a loan. Alice helped me to draw up a business plan and everything is costed out. If it comes to asking for a loan, I hope it impresses them.'

Her voice bubbles with enthusiasm. This is a different Hanna: happy, keen... a Hanna I can like. She smiles at me again – that's twice within a few seconds – and I smile back.

'I'm hoping to make enough money so I can get a place of my own. The business is my number one ambition but getting the hell out of this house comes a close second.'

She wants to leave. To give up life in her luxurious home and support herself. Unless she's phenomenally lucky, it's a huge gamble.

She glances up the corridor. 'You should get to the office, or you'll have my pain of a father on your back.'

She's right; I was a no-show last night and now I'm late for work with no excuse at the ready. If Max asks, I'll have to wing it.

A walk up the corridor takes me to my office door. *My office.* Just a couple of days ago, who'd have thought it?

As I walk in, I immediately see Tara, head down, shuffling papers on what is now my desk. She looks up and smiles. That usually immaculate blonde hair is flopping over her forehead. This is not the bad-tempered Tara who met me at the door earlier. Her mood has had a complete turnaround.

'Sorry, Donna, I wouldn't invade your space unless it was urgent.'

More smiles, and I nod back. She's walking up and down the office, shifting things and looking in drawers.

'Perhaps I can help?'

'I'm looking for a document that came in by email last week. It's from a customer in London. He wants to buy one of our houses near here. I can't afford to let him down. Max printed out two copies. He left one on this desk to be forwarded to the company solicitor and the second copy on my desk. Both copies are missing.'

She flicks her hair back and fixes it behind her ears and looks directly at me.

'I wish he'd at least try to get things right. He should be in here tearing the place apart himself but he's resting. *Resting!* I wish I could be so indulgent. He told me his leg is playing up, an old skiing accident. He broke his femur and had to have an operation. His leg is full of metal now and gives him pain at times.'

I feel for him; the knock-on effect of such an injury can't be much fun. I would offer to look for the missing email, but both my desk and the floor are covered with papers.

'I want to know what happened to the copy I left on your desk, Donna. Have you put it somewhere, perhaps for safe keeping? Have you let Hanna come in here? She'd do anything to upset me.'

How to respond to that one? She can't really think it's down to me. This is the first time I've set foot in here since she showed me round. As for Hanna, why would she move it?

'I've no idea what's happened to the document.' Firm voice is fully in gear. 'The desk has only been mine since this morning and I've not even sat at it yet.'

I'm trying to make a point. Not very successfully as she completely ignores my reasoning and continues to litter the floor with yet more paperwork.

'Missing documents are a serious matter. This sort of sloppiness isn't good enough, Donna. This job demands you take responsibility for what goes on in here.'

I'm mystified. How can she think this has anything to do with me? She's not thinking straight. A missing printout, important and needed urgently, I understand her frustration, but what does she expect me to do? If this is typical Tara, I'll quickly get pissed off with this behaviour.

'Tara, this is my first time in here. Whatever is missing is not my fault. But I can help you look,' I say surveying the mess and wondering where to start.

'Everything that happens in here is your responsibility.'

She's smiling again. I can't tell if she's angry or not.

'I don't want hiring you to be a big mistake.'

A big mistake! I've done nothing wrong. If anything, she's the one making mistakes, not me.

'You could print the email out again.'

It seems the logical solution to me. But Tara doesn't see it that way. She shakes her head, looks at me and tuts.

'I'm not stupid,' she says calmly. 'It's obvious to me that it's been deliberately deleted, and the printouts destroyed.'

She stops leaning on the desk and stands up straight.

'All I ask is that people do their job and don't cock it up.'

I want to protest again but bite it back. In her eyes I'm to blame and that's that.

'This could be down to Hanna, up to her tricks again. She's done this sort of thing before but this time she's gone too far.'

Why would Hanna deliberately hide things from her parents? It didn't make sense, and anyway, Tara locked the door after she'd shown me around, so she couldn't have got into the office. On the other hand, Hanna is more than capable of getting her sticky fingers on the key. But what has she got to gain by deleting emails and stealing papers?

Tara has created mayhem, but it'll be me who has to restore some sort of order, and I haven't a clue what goes where. As for the problem of the email, I don't have enough computer knowledge to offer a solution, so best not to try.

'You've been no help at all, Donna,' Tara tells me. 'I hope you put that right and quick. When I want something, I expect it to be on hand and given to me within minutes.'

Now it's a condescending look and a half-hearted smile. I suppose I should be grateful. The mood she's in, Tara could have seriously lost it, but she's kept her anger under control.

'What I need is someone in this office who is capable, who has answers, an assistant who can make things run smoothly... Instead, I've got you.'

Have I made a terrible mistake in coming here?

NINE

Not a good start to my new job, but it's taught me a lesson. If something goes wrong or interferes with the smooth running of Max's business, Tara is quick to point the finger, and right now that's at me.

She walks out of the office, says nothing, not even an apology for being so unreasonable or for leaving a total mess behind her. I thought I was working for Max but it would seem I'm to be at the beck and call of both of them.

I start the thankless task of scooping up the papers and folders off the floor. I plonk them on top of a row of cabinets. They can wait until later when I've calmed down.

I'm sat at my desk without a clue what to do. Pack my stuff and get the hell out of here and not look back? It's tempting, and I doubt they'll miss me. I feel like a spare part anyway.

'D'you think she's trying to tell you something?'

It was Hanna, back again like a bad penny. She didn't even knock, just walked straight in. She's heard her mother behaving like a witch from hell and is here to rub my nose in it.

'What did I tell you? The pair of them are bad news.'

The last thing I need right now is Hanna round my neck. I

have to get rid of her. 'I can't talk now.' I point at the cabinets. 'If I'm to do any work today, I'll have to sort this little lot first.'

Hanna folds her arms and nods. 'Tara doesn't do things by halves. Want a hand?'

'Thanks, but I'll manage.'

'Suit yourself but this won't stop. She can't help herself. Be warned: if she doesn't lose her temper, the cool, calm version of Tara is just as dangerous.'

This isn't Hanna joking around; this is serious Hanna, a girl who means every word and knows Tara much better than me. But *dangerous*, surely not.

I watch her eyes flick around the room before she fixes them on the door.

'We'd better talk quietly,' she whispers. 'She could be listening to us.'

Just in case, I creep to the door and take a look up and down the corridor. I stand on tiptoe and take a peek in Max's office. It's empty. There's no one hanging around. 'It's safe to talk,' I tell her.

'She used to give Alice a hard time. She never raised her voice, never swore; all the criticism and the treats were always delivered in an understated way.'

'She gave me a right dressing down,' I tell her. 'How did Alice cope?

'When she first started here, Tara tried the missing document scam with her as well. She was upset, almost on the point of giving up, but when Tara realised she'd gone too far, she changed her tune and managed to talk her into staying.'

'What did Alice do about it, long term?'

'She found out stuff, bad stuff about the pair of them but particularly about Max.'

'What kind of bad stuff? What did she find out?'

'She wouldn't say, and believe me, I asked often enough. But once, when Tara had been particularly awful, Alice stood her corner and let slip the word *police*. From that day forward things never got out of hand again. Tara was all sweetness, Max toed the line, and Alice was much happier.'

My ears prick up. Exactly what did Alice have on the pair, and how did she find out about whatever it was? It must be something big if it had the power to stop all this nonsense. Another thought occurs to me. Whatever Alice knew might help me get some answers. I'm not sure how, that depends on what it is, but I've got to make progress. The questions thrown up by the funeral are still there. The problem is this family, this house and the job have managed to hijack my brain. If I'm not careful I'll forget the real reason I'm here in the first place.

What Alice discovered about Max could be anything, but if Alice threatened them with the police, a few possibilities occur to me. A problem with the business, perhaps. Alice must have known what went on, the good and the bad. She did the accounts, so it could be shady money; for example, is Max fiddling his taxes or even guilty of embezzlement? This is ridiculous, my imagination is running away with me; it won't be anything like that.

'I need to take a leaf out of Alice's book and find something to keep Tara off my back,' I tell Hanna. 'This job, and the accommodation that comes with it, are the answer to my prayers, but there are limits to what I'll put up with. Getting the blame for anything going wrong in here when it's nothing to do with me, for example. If it happens again, I'll leave so fast my feet won't touch. Help me with this, Hanna, and I'll owe you.'

I'm a bloody fool. What've I said? The girl might ask for anything, and what I've got to offer is strictly limited. There's an annoying silence. Time to make myself clear, make her understand how serious this is for me.

'I need this job and everything that goes with it, but tetchy Tara isn't part of the deal.'

'Tetchy Tara,' she says, grinning. 'I like it.'

Hanna might like it, but I don't. I can't work like this. Living on my nerves, afraid that at any minute Tara could burst into my office and mess with my head. It's barely ten in the morning and I'm sick of the day already. If this is the norm, I'll be exhausted within a week.

'Come on, Hanna. Give me something I can use.'

'For starters neither of them are what they seem. The clothes, the car, this house... they're all a front. Max has at least one dirty little secret: his mistress, Isabel. Not that she's such a secret these days. But Alice said there was something else, something in their past they do not want to come out. I asked Alice why she threatened Tara with the police but she wouldn't tell me.'

We've all got stuff in the past we want to keep secret; I know that better than most. But what have the glamourous Max and Tara got to hide?

'I need money, Donna. Enough to start my business and make a fresh start. I'm desperate to get out of this shithole.'

'That's heavy stuff, Hanna. The business you want to open will take a lot of money. You are dependent on your father coughing up. What if he won't? If your father won't help, then your best bet is the bank. Why not go and talk to someone, see what they're prepared to offer you.'

'That'll take too long. I need the money now, Donna. The thing is, I know you can get it for me.'

She's dreaming if she thinks that. 'Sorry but I'm broke. All I've got is a couple of pounds in my pocket to last until pay day. Why d'you think I took this job?'

'I know it has nothing to do with money.'

Now I'm on alert. Why did she say that? Does she know something or was that a lucky guess?

'That's rubbish. Like you, I need money too. That's the only reason I'm here.'

My face is hot; it'll have gone a deep shade of crimson. Another manifestation of my inability to lie and be convincing.

'I know you're lying. This job is a means to an end. You've got questions that need answers. No matter how weird my parents' behaviour is, you won't leave until you get them.'

She's spot on. That was not a lucky guess. Logic tells me that there's no way she can know the truth, not unless she played a part in setting this Alice thing up. A scary thought and not something I want to get into right now.

'I've no money so you're wasting your time even asking. I'm never likely to have the amount you need either. Tell me Alice's little secret or Tara's behaviour will drive me away.'

She shakes her head and those eyes cloud over. She wants me to stay and that gives me a lever.

'I won't survive if you go.'

A bit dramatic even for Hanna. I want to tell her not to be silly, but her eyes are shiny with tears. She's serious, but why she thinks like that is beyond me.

'Of course you'll survive, Hanna. You're not in any danger. You live with your parents; they won't let any harm come to you.'

'You know nothing. I live on my nerves, I never know what's coming next.'

'I can't listen to any more of this fantasy, Hanna. You are one lucky girl. There's plenty out there who'd give their eyeteeth to be in your position.'

Hanna perches on the end of my desk. She plays around with my computer mouse for a few seconds; perhaps it helps her to think. Tossing the thing aside she looks at me and nods.

'I've no idea what it was that Alice found out. But my parents don't know that. It was just the mere mention of the police that frightened Max. You can use that, twist the words, make him think that you do know.'

'I'm not a good liar, Hanna, no way can I pull that one off.

Alice knew something; she must have given Max a clue what that was. I've got nothing.'

'Whatever Alice knew was juicy enough to scare Max, and it worked like a charm. He didn't say a word out of place after that. She told me it amused her no end to watch him squirm. You can do it, Donna, make him pay for your silence too. Between the two of us we could get all of the money we both need.'

I don't comment on that one. The last thing I want is to be in cahoots with Hanna. It's too risky; she is their daughter, after all.

'Did Alice give you any hint at all about what she knew?'

'No, but she might have done if she hadn't died.'

'How old was Alice?'

'Forty-two, we went out for a meal on her birthday. Max bought her a gold necklace. Generous because he's not one to splash out on gifts. At Christmas it's tins of biscuits and chocolates all round. He spends a tenner on everyone at most. Just goes to show the power Alice had over the pair of them.'

'How did Alice die? Had she been ill?' I couldn't get any details out of either Max or Tara but Hanna may be more forthcoming.

'It was a stupid accident that killed her. She must have tripped and fell down the stairs,' Hanna tells me.

'*Must have*. Does that mean no one actually saw what happened?'

'Tara was in the kitchen talking to Maria.'

'And Max?'

'He was out, I think.'

Hanna pulls a face and shrugs. 'What does it matter anyway who was here? The coroner said *accident*, so that's that. No blame was attached to anyone.

I shudder. I can't help it; the woman, fit and healthy, died in this house. That very day she would have been sat at my desk.

'Max was so upset. He was weird for days, hardly said anything to me or Tara. He was out every night with Isabel and was drunk more than he was sober.'

'It was a terrible thing to happen. I'm not surprised he was upset and reacted badly.'

'Drop it, Donna, it happened, it's over, and the woman is six feet under. Max can be emotional, but he soon bounces back. Seeing Isabel helped him get over the incident. Tara was useless, too tearful to be of any use to anyone.'

Isabel: she was the woman making the rude comments about me at the funeral. She's attractive but not in Tara's league. With her as a wife, it's hard to imagine Max wanting anyone else.

'Where does Isabel work?'

'She's an accountant at some firm in Manchester, but mostly she works from home. Might as well not bother, the time she spends at the gym and having lunch with her cronies.'

'Well, what d'you think? The info I've given you must be worth something.'

'I've already told you, I'm broke, and you haven't actually told me anything. I can't use a vague idea that Max and Tara are up to something as a threat. I need facts – then I'll be in with a chance.'

'Okay, if you've got no money then you'll have to pay me in some other way. The lowdown on Max's business will do. Whatever Alice knew must be something to do with it. She spent most of her time with her head stuck in those accounts. You'll find out all sorts of stuff yourself working in this office. Anything you think is odd, tell me.'

'What are you expecting me to find?'

'Info on something illegal he's into or anything he'd want kept quiet. Find out what it is, and I'll owe you.'

Hanna believes her father is into something illegal, but I doubt it. Max runs a successful business; he has no need to cheat. The best I can offer is to keep a wary eye out, but even if I do find anything out, I'll be reluctant to tell Hanna.

'I'm not wrong, Donna. I've been watching and listening for months. Max gets phone calls day and night, strangers come to the door after dark. He never explains why or invites them inside. When he gets these calls it's to a different mobile, not the one he always uses. Alice was suspicious too.'

This is my first day in this office, and I know next to nothing about Max's business, but instinctively I feel that Hanna is wrong, that this is sour grapes. At best I'll have access to the accounts package, a few spreadsheets and emails. If there is something wrong, and that's a big if, it is bound to take me some time and more knowledge than I have to find it. Simply looking at this house suggests that there is no shortage of money. Max doesn't need to do anything illegal; the business appears to provide everything this family wants and more.

'I can't do what you want, Hanna, I can't spy on your dad.'

'Course you can, it's easy. You find a document, email, or entry on the spreadsheets that looks suspicious. You photocopy it and pass it to me.'

She's asking the impossible. This job is new, I'm unfamiliar with the paperwork, the routine, I'll mess up. I don't want this conversation. What I do want is the girl off my back but she's not taking the hint.

She rolls those intense blue eyes at me. 'Please think about it. I need your help.'

Ignoring her, I start sorting the papers on my desk. Hanna has outstayed her welcome and I want rid of her. A few minutes' silence seems to work.

'Okay, I'll leave you in peace, but we will talk about this again. I'm disappointed in you, Donna, you're missing a trick. We get something big on Max and he'll pay us to keep us quiet. I need the money and so do you. You've had it hard these last years, living on the breadline, staying away from people who want to harm you. I thought you'd have more balls.'

Her parting shot as she leaves the office sends a shiver down my spine. I've told no one about how much of a recluse I've become or the reason why. This young woman, a stranger I've never met before, knows more about me than is comfortable. Just how much more does she know, and who has told her?

TEN

More balls. She's got some cheek. I have had a hard time; that's life struggling on your own at only sixteen years old. My experience hasn't made me weak, it's made me strong. The girl has no idea.

Hanna has only been gone a few minutes when I hear the slam of Max's office door. What now? I'm expecting Tara, coming to have another go, but it isn't her who comes through the door; it's Max.

'I'm sorry, Donna.'

He's standing on the other side of my desk, his eyes fixed on mine as he runs a hand through that thick dark hair of his. God, he's tall, and the white shirt on his back fits so well I bet it's handmade to his measurements. I'm trying not to blush, not to be tongue-tied, but failing horribly. Max is a married man, and even if he wasn't, no way would he fancy me.

As for the apology, he's not the one at fault; his wife is, but at this moment, even if he was, I could forgive him anything.

'Tara's behaviour was unacceptable. This is your first day and you get the blame for something that can't possibly be down to you. I promise it won't happen again.'

He gives me a smile that makes me shiver. Hanna reckons he has a mistress. Looking at him now, I can well understand why any woman would fall for him.

'No matter, I've got broad shoulders,' is my reply. 'A missing document when you need it is annoying.'

'It still doesn't excuse her attitude. I stepped in, had another look through the mail folders and found what she wanted in the recycle bin.'

He has apologised for Tara and we do have to work together. I decide to let her off this time; it's better for all of us if we're not at loggerheads. I watch him as he surveys the mess she's made. No mention of helping to clear it up though.

'What do you want doing today? I'm all set to make a start.'

'I've got a couple of emails, and several invoices to enter into the accounts package we use. Alice always entered them onto one of her spreadsheets too, for backup. She was nothing if not thorough.' He hands over two folders. 'You'll find them in there. Invoices given to customers and those that came in from suppliers.'

'When you're done, stick them in those two cabinets by the wall in customer name order. Once a month Alice reconciled the lot and sorted any errors. If there were any unpaid invoices from customers, she chased them up. The amounts owing can be eye-watering at times. We sell several houses to agents at a time and need prompt payment or it's us in trouble. There's no need to stress about anything. The accounts are simple enough, thanks to Alice.'

But it's still a responsibility. I've experienced one of Tara's tantrums and I don't want a repeat performance. He hands me a slip of paper; written on it are log-in details for my laptop.

'If you need anything else just knock on my office door and I'll sort it.'

As Max leaves, his hand brushes against my shoulder. On purpose, or an accidental gesture? Either way, it's unsettling. In that instance I doubt I can threaten him with anything, especially not snitch to Tara or the police if me and Hanna find something. I don't want to put him through that. He needs to watch his step though; he's taking a risk with Isabel.

He's about to go through the door when he turns and says, 'I thought we could all go out for a meal tonight. As an apology for making your first day a nightmare. Lakeside, on the edge of the village, does wonderful food. What d'you think?'

What do I think? Flattered to be invited is my first thought.

'Great, we'll leave at eight.'

A quick nod of his head and he's gone. This has to stop. I'm going to see the man every day and I can't go all gaga each time he talks to me.

He's only been gone minutes when Hanna's back. I watch her eyes flick over the floor and wait for the sarcastic comment about her mother.

'No offer to pick this little lot up then? Tara is good at creating chaos, and Max ignores the mess she leaves behind.'

'It doesn't matter, I'll get stuck in and have it sorted by lunchtime.'

'I heard him talking about a meal out. That's about the pair of them getting back in your good books. Don't be taken in; Max can turn on the charm as easily as turning on a tap.'

'I think it's good of him. He's trying to put things right after Tara's outburst this morning, that's all.'

'What will you wear? Lakeside is on the posh side. Have you got something suitable?'

Sadly I don't have anything good enough for a fancy restaurant in this neck of the woods, unlike Tara, who will look fabulous, whereas I'll look like the home help.

'If you like, I can lend you something.'

I say nothing but the problem is obvious to both of us. Hanna is only a couple of years younger than me but is much taller and at least three sizes bigger. From the look on her face, she must have read my mind.

'I know what you're thinking but we can't all be stick insects like you.'

She looks hurt and I immediately feel guilty.

'Relax, Donna, if you don't fancy anything of mine there's an entire room full of clothes Tara doesn't wear anymore. Take one of her dresses. She won't mind because she won't even recognise it. She'll have worn it once, if at all.'

It's kind of Hanna to come to my rescue, but there's no way that she can be sure that Tara won't recognise it. If she does, it will be mega embarrassing. She might even make a scene in public. On the other hand, this is the first time I've been out with the family, and I want to make a good impression but not at the expense of being dragged over the coals by Tara.

'I'll come and have a look at your wardrobe during my lunch hour if you're free. As for Tara's stuff, I'd rather not risk it.'

She shrugs. 'Please yourself.'

I will give whatever she has in her wardrobe a look but I'm doubtful that I'll take anything.

Once she's left the office, I look at the mess on the floor. I'll pick that lot up later. I'm keen to have a snoop around, to take a look at what was Alice's domain. First, the contents of the cabinets, the stuff that's not on the floor, that is. The desk drawers are a must too. It's possible that Alice kept her own personal things in there.

It takes only five minutes for me to realise that I'm wasting my time. The desk drawers are empty apart from pens and paper clips, and the cabinets are mostly empty too. Not surprising as the folders they contained are now decorating the floor along with the paperwork they had in them.

Time to log on to the computer system. There could be things saved there that will give me answers to the questions burning a hole in my brain. Apart from which I've got to get used to working with it and need to brush up on my skills. I've used computers before on the course I was sent on, but that wasn't the real world. Mess this up and I'll have Tara on my back big style. Leaving me responsible for this aspect of the business is risky. No one has shown me the ropes so I'm not sure what I'm doing. On the screen is the icon to open the accounts, and there are several folders labelled *spreadsheets* and one for bank statements. I'm surprised I've been given access to these, but if Max is happy with it then who am I to raise questions?

After a quick look around, I decide everything does look straightforward enough even for me. The accounts software looks simple to use and Alice had set up two important spreadsheets, one for income, the other for expenditure.

I click on the income one and the first thing that strikes me is the huge amount of money that Max's business earns. He is in the business of building and selling houses, and I can see from the accounts that nearly fifty have sold in the past month. I'd have expected the figures to be good but Max is raking in an absolute fortune. I'm not surprised that this family has a luxury lifestyle.

I feel more relaxed about the job now. Max is right; the accounts are simple enough to deal with. I get this right and the experience will be useful, something I can use when I'm looking for another job. When I get answers to the Alice problem, I'll be out of here. I haven't given any thought to what I'll do, but I should. I can't go back to Ella; that wouldn't be fair. I will need a job and somewhere to live. I've already decided to save every penny I earn here. Solving the Alice problem isn't going to be as quick as I'd thought, so I may as well make the most of it.

I feel better now, more positive. I stretch out my arms, flex my fingers, and my elbows send a pile of paperwork spinning to the floor. My stomach churns and I feel the usual flush of embarrassment hit my face. Stupid because no one can see what's happened. It's no big deal anyway, the floor is already covered in papers. I'm about to start the job of picking it all up and putting everything back in the cabinets. This little lot won't make much difference.

If I stay, continue with the job and try to integrate with this family, I must learn not to panic at every mistake I make. Moving the chair out of the way, I get down on all fours to retrieve what's scattered under the desk. Once I've got things tidy, I'll have some lunch.

I'm crawling under my desk, scooping up papers, when I spot it.

Taped to the underside of my desk is a memory stick with my name on it. I stare at it for several seconds, debating what to do. Did Alice hide it there? And who was she hiding it from?

I'm on my hands and knees squinting at the underside of the desk, but even in this uncomfortable position I can see the tape holding the thing in place has my name on it. *Donna Slade* written in red felt tip.

This cannot be happening. Donna is invisible, she exists only in the shadows. It's impossible for anyone in this house to know me. But the proof that someone does is staring me in the face. The memory stick was deliberately left for me to find; it's no surprise that my hands are shaking.

ELEVEN

My stomach hasn't had time to settle from Tara's attack earlier, and now it's doing somersaults again. For someone to hide the stick like this, the contents have to be important, but to who? Me, perhaps; it might hold the answer to why I'm here. I'd certainly welcome that. Or it could be the lowdown on Max, particularly as he may have crossed a line legally, or so his daughter reckons.

First there'd been the horror of seeing my real name on the coffin and now the name Donna on this. Both important names to me but only I know that. Something is very wrong. Knowing me as Donna is one thing, but is it likely that anyone would know both? Does someone in this house know more about me than they should? Even if that someone was Alice, how does that work?

Pulling the stick free, I scramble over to my chair and examine the thing. A shiver slips down my back. I'm spooked. Someone, surely Alice, must have hidden the stick there knowing I'd find it. I can't for the life of me understand how they could be so certain the right sequence of events would ensure that I did. Find out what's on it and you'll know why, common sense tells me. Dare I look? Of course I can. I have every right.

I remove the tape and slide the stick into the computer's USB port. The screen flickers to life, making my nerves even worse. Stupid, I know, but it's what I'll find that scares me. Images, documents, or perhaps something more sinister? It's too late now, the deed is done. I shut my eyes, not daring to look. But the truth is far less frightening than I imagined. A huge disappointment, in fact.

The memory stick is password-protected.

Intended for me but I can't read it; it doesn't make sense. The problems thrown my way are annoying and fast adding up. I'm getting nowhere with solving my original problem: who was the Alice who'd taken my name, and why had she done that? I'm rapidly getting sick and tired of the entire situation and wonder yet again if it's time to throw in the towel.

Putting the stick and tape in my jeans pocket, I leave my desk, lock the office door, and go to my rooms. I need time on my own to think. If I do decide to leave, it will have implications. I'll never find out the truth, for a start. Could I live with that? Possibly. It's not as if the problem is life-threatening or anything. Who am I kidding? I leave now and the mystery of Alice will be with me for the rest of my days. For my own sanity I have no choice but to stay.

'Early finish?'

I jump as Hanna catches up with me. My heart sinks. Just when I could do without her. She is another reason to grab my stuff and run. She's not going to drop the idea that I owe her.

'If you're free you can have a look at a dress I've picked out for you. I think it will suit you, but if you don't like it choose anything you like.'

It's generous of her to help me this way, and now I feel guilty for wanting rid of her.

'Okay'—I nod with a smile—'lead the way.'

She doesn't say a word as the two of us walk down the corridor towards the door of her domain. We stand outside one of two doors next to each other.

'This is my room. It has my name on it, see?' She taps the nameplate.

Fair enough, but the door next to it has her name on it too.

'That door is locked and it's got to stay that way.'

The obvious question is why, but do I really want to know?

'No one goes in there except me, and then only if I have to.'

'You could have your very own sitting room like me. You'd have your own space. Don't you fancy that?'

'Not in that room, I don't. I never go in there and I don't want anyone else to either.'

'Okay,' I say, with a nod. 'Not a problem.'

I want to ask what the mystery is but bite the question back; I've enough of my own to solve.

'What's behind that door still gives me nightmares,' Hanna tells me with no explanation. 'It was my room for a long time before I decided I'd had enough and moved in here.'

She's got tears in her eyes. She won't tell me what's wrong, so I can't help her. The conversation is getting tricky, entering realms I don't like. Hanna is one complicated young woman; even with my background I'm not as mixed up as she is.

'You nearly always refer to your parents by their first names. Is there a reason for that?'

She looks me up and down as if I'm stupid for asking.

'They don't deserve anything else, certainly not *Mum and Dad*.' She shrugs her shoulders and folds her arms. 'It doesn't seem to bother them. More proof if needed that they don't give a damn. They are too wrapped up in their own world to care what happens to me or how I feel.'

This isn't what I wanted. I've walked into a domestic shambles littered with secrets and lies. Once I'm through the door, my eyes wander to the dress lying on her bed. It's dreadful, a sludge-grey colour with a high neck, flared skirt and far too big for me.

'Take it away and try it on if you want.'

I don't have much choice; she is trying to help, and telling her what I really think would upset her even more.

'Thanks, as long as you're sure.'

'If you like it, keep the thing, I'll never wear it again. I've put on far too much weight so I don't think it'll ever fit me again.'

I pick up the dress, the fabric is thick and scratchy. There's no way I can wear this, but I've no idea what explanation to give to Hanna that won't upset her. But this dress is going to the back of my wardrobe and will not see the light of day again.

'Take this, you might need it.'

She throws me a black clutch bag. My friend Ella had given me a pair of black patent heels as a parting present. Shoes that actually fit me, not like the ones I'd worn to the funeral. The bag will go nicely; it's just a shame about the dress.

'Thanks for the loan, I appreciate it. I've never worn anything remotely like this dress before.' And I'm not joking.

Hanna's reply, another shrug. 'Take it, make Tara sit up and take notice. She'll be as jealous as hell seeing you look good.'

Tara, jealous of me? Not a chance.

TWELVE

I'm nervous about the night ahead and what might happen. A flash restaurant and nothing to wear is my worst nightmare. It was good of Hanna to lend me her dress but there's no way I can wear it, I'll look a fright.

What's the use pretending, I'll have to cry off, tell the others I've got a migraine or something. I hope that Max and Tara accept the excuse; otherwise I'll have to deal with more of Tara's disapproval.

There's a knock on the door and I pray it's not Hanna again. The last hour has worn me out.

'Donna, are you there?'

Max is standing in my doorway, an apologetic smile on his face.

'I'm sorry, Donna, but I couldn't help but overhear your conversation with Hanna earlier.'

Does he often earwig on other's conversations? I wonder. If so then I'll have to watch what I say about him.

'I should have been more sensitive when I invited you to join us for dinner in one of the most exclusive restaurants around here without a thought about what you might wear.'

A bit personal, but on the other hand, he's right. I point to the dress on the sofa. 'Hanna kindly lent me something.'

'No way,' he laughs. 'I don't doubt she meant well, but, honestly, you can't wear *that*.'

'I don't have much choice, Max. I've not had any spare money to spend on clothes recently.' I've tempered my reply; if I tell Max that I haven't bought anything new for three years, all I'll get is pity, and I can't cope with that.

'Let me help. Tara has a room full of clothes she no longer wears. You can take your pick, she won't mind.'

'Can I ask her, make sure?'

'She's out this afternoon getting preened at the hairdresser. Don't worry, it'll be fine. Tara will be pleased to help.'

I highly doubt that. If I turn up wearing one of her dresses, she's bound to say something. I don't want a scene in public, but what choice do I have? I'll look dreadful in what Hanna gave me.

'It's fine, I know Tara will be happy to help. Come on, I'll show you.'

One charming smile is all it takes. I'm following him up the stairs towards his and Tara's bedroom. Thankfully, we don't go in. I don't want to see where they sleep; that's all a bit too intimate for me. Instead, Max opens the next door and ushers me in.

The room contains nothing but rails of clothes. Everything, dresses casual and formal, skirts, blouses and winter stuff, including two fur coats. Genuine, I wonder, stroking one with the palm of my hand.

Max takes hold of a rail and pulls it towards me. 'Going-out dresses are here. Have a rummage, choose one you like and it's yours for the evening.'

I'm embarrassed because Max is watching me. I feel as if his eyes are boring into my back.

'I'm no expert but this colour would suit you perfectly,' he says, selecting a beautiful blue silk dress. Tight fitting, with a low neckline and a split up the side, it leaves very little to the imagination. He hands it to me and nods.

'This will suit you, I'm sure. It'll go well with that lovely red hair.'

Now I am embarrassed.

'See, it's never even been worn, the price tag is still on it, so Tara won't mind.'

I catch my breath as I see how much it cost, a small fortune in the world of Donna.

Flattering but optimistic, these days I doubt I'd look gorgeous in anything, but the dress is far more suitable for the evening than Hanna's offering.

'Take it, try it on. If you're not happy, come and find me and we'll look again.'

I don't know what to say. I take the dress and give him a grin. I bet I look stupid; a simple thank you would have done. Instead, I must look like a small child being handed a bag of sweets.

'Accessories?' he asks.

Will the shoes Ella gave me work? Not with this dress, I decide.

'How about these?'

Max hands me a pair of navy blue high heels and a clutch to match; they'll fit the bill perfectly.

He picks up a jewellery box and searches through it.

'Borrow these as well. They are the perfect finishing touch.'

He hands me a lovely pearl necklace. It's all too much and I'm about to protest, but he stops me.

'I wouldn't offer if I wasn't sure Tara would be okay with it.'

The dress, the shoes and bag, and now the necklace, I couldn't have wished for better. Max is a lifesaver.

'Thanks, Max, this is kind of you. You've helped me out of a tricky situation. Without it, I'd have had no choice but to come along in my jeans and trainers.'

'No worries. You'll look knock-out and I'm sure we'll have a great night.

Getting dressed up for a posh night out is a new experience for me; even so, being done up like a dog's dinner doesn't help my acute case of the jitters. I'm desperate to get this right, not to make a fool of myself, especially not in front of Max.

Get a grip, girl, this is stupid. Max doesn't fancy you; he's just trying to help.

Back in my rooms, I take a shower and do what I can to make my hair look decent. It's long and a deep red colour. I've never liked it. At school I was teased mercilessly and now would dye it some other colour if I could afford it. I put that on my mental list of things to put right, along with buying some decent clothes. As kind as Max is, I don't want him to bail me out again; it's embarrassing.

Hair dried and smoothed down as much as I can, I'm wearing the fabulous dress with the pearls, and I stare at my reflection in the full-length mirror. I'm thin, which is a shame because this dress deserves curves. I used to have a good figure but not anymore; now I'm all skin and bones, as my aunt would have said. It's going to take a while to put the pounds back on and restore things to how they used to be. I'd love to give Tara a run for her money but there's no chance of that. I pull a face at my reflection; not in a million years can I compete with her.

I wonder how Hanna feels when she gets ready for a night out. What she thinks when she looks at herself in the mirror. I don't mean to be unkind, but I doubt anything she does in terms of clothes or hairstyle will make much difference. She's a young woman with her entire life in front of her. I'd like to help, but she'll only take it the wrong way. Best keep well out of it.

I should move it. Too much thinking about Hanna and getting ready have eaten into the evening. I'd like to put some make-up on, but I don't have any. These last years I haven't bothered with my appearance. I've been too busy keeping body and soul together but now things are different. Soon I will have both the money and security to spend a little on myself. Make-up or not, tonight I still look better than I would have without Max's help. Better by far than having to manage with what I've got, which, let's face it, is next to nothing.

Improving how I look is all very well, but the money I earn must first be put towards restarting my life. I intend to save enough for a deposit on a flat, somewhere new, away from the city. A place where I don't have to be anonymous and can make friends and have a social life.

Posing in front of the full-length mirror again, I run my hands down my figure. You don't look half bad, Donna dear, I tell myself. Now go and enjoy yourself.

I've never been to a restaurant like Lakeside before. The excitement I felt earlier is fast diminishing, replaced by the good old nerves.

You'll be okay, Donna. That's probably right but this family is unpredictable. The evening could become a disaster in a heartbeat.

Deep breath, and I'm primed and ready to meet the others at the front door as arranged, but only Hanna is waiting.

'You're not wearing the dress,' she says, her body language deflated.

'Sorry, Hanna, but it was a little too big. The length, you see, the skirt was down to my ankles.' A lie but I don't want to hurt her feelings.

'They've had to go ahead, make sure their table isn't given to someone else. The one they've reserved is by the window with a fabulous view of the lake, but the girl who takes the bookings is notorious for not writing these things down.'

Hanna makes no further comments about how I'm dressed and I don't invite any. She is wearing a black dress that doesn't quite feel right for the occasion, which is a surprise when she made such a fuss about what I was going to wear. I'm learning that everything in this family is a contradiction.

'The taxi Max ordered for us is here.' She smiles. 'Ten minutes down the road and we'll be there. You'll love the food; I know I do. Problem is I tend to like food a bit too much,' she admits. 'Indian food especially, also the fare from that new Thai place on the high street.' She tilts her head to one side. 'It's educational, you know. You learn a lot about other countries from the food they eat.'

When Hanna stops talking, the mood seems to change, and I notice her bottom lip quivering. She looks close to tears.

'Are you okay, Hanna? What's wrong?'

She looks me in the eye. 'I'm not stupid, I know what everyone thinks when they look at me. Nobody can see past the fat body.'

'Oh, Hanna, that's not the case at all. You're beautiful.'

'Everyone thinks I eat all the wrong food and that's why I look like a beached whale.'

How to answer that one?

'That's not true. You look lovely. So where else d'you eat?' I ask lightly.

'There's a Mexican place a couple of miles away. We go there occasionally. Before you ask, I'm not too keen on the food there, so I don't eat like a pig, and I do know from experience how pigs can eat.'

'Does Tara ever cook?' Too critical? My tone suggests as much. I'm already in hot water and treading on eggshells.

'Tara can't cook,' is her blunt reply. 'We have Maria to do that. She lives in the village, does the cooking and orders the grocery deliveries. Tara can't be bothered to shop either. I don't think she's ever seen the inside of a supermarket. Maria tries but I don't like what she cooks much, too plain and wholesome for me. It's all salad, fish, and more yukky stuff. I throw most of it in the bin. Give me the chippy or a good foreign restaurant any day.'

I want to ask more questions but I hold my tongue. Hanna doesn't invite more talk but sits quietly, staring out of the taxi window.

The driver pulls into the restaurant car park. I strain my neck trying to glimpse inside. Exclusive means money, and this is another example of how the other half live, but I'm disappointed. This is the front of the restaurant and the blinds are closed. Not surprising: who wants to look out at a car park?

'I promise you none of this is down to me,' she says, which immediately unnerves me. I've no idea what she's talking about, but from the look on her face, whatever it is has got her rattled.

'I have my orders; I was told to get the taxi with you and make sure you go inside. I'm sorry, Donna, this is the last thing I want, but I have to do as I'm told.'

I've no idea what she means. *Orders*, that could mean anything, but I can do without another puzzle; it's not good for my already strung-out nerves. I look her in the eye. Hanna is good at hiding her emotions, but there are tears in her eyes. She allows her parents to walk all over her and doesn't let them see how she feels. I'm different it would seem. The tears are a give-away that something is wrong, something she knows involves me. I'm not in the mood, but whatever it is, I'll give as good as I get. Grabbing the clutch bag firmly in my hand, I get out of the taxi.

'Okay, no worries. I'll see you in there.'

'The locals are a nosey bunch and you're new in the area so be prepared to get stared at,' is her parting shot as I close the taxi door behind me.

It turns out she's right but not for any of the reasons flitting through my head. New girl on the block – might even find me attractive.

I spot Max and Tara straight away, and instantly know I've

made a mistake coming out tonight. The pair are sat at a window table with a view of the lake, just as Hanna had said. Max looks splendid in his dark suit, white shirt and bow tie. It's Tara who puts my head in a spin.

We are both wearing exactly the same dress; in fact, I'm done up *exactly* like her. The dress, the shoes, even down to the string of pearls around my neck. I've been set up.

THIRTEEN

This will be a major embarrassment for Tara, a situation like this is a nightmare for a woman like her. Her clothes are expensive, many of her things a one-off. There will be people here who know her and will find the situation amusing. Part of me wants to turn and run, take the taxi back to the house and forget this ever happened. But I can't. I'm angry, and need to find out why Max did this to me. What game is he playing?

People are already looking at the pair of us, pointing and whispering. Max has engineered this. He must have known what Tara planned to wear and he made sure I mirrored her in every way. Now I know why the price tag was still hanging around the neckline of this one. He must have bought it from the same designer shop.

As I walk closer, Tara gets to her feet, her face a mix of shock and upset.

'What the hell is this?'

The words are aimed at Max, not me. Something of a relief as I'm the innocent party.

'Calm down, Tara. It's a simple mistake, that's all.'

Some mistake. Tara and I are done up like twin dolls. Max has planned this to perfection. What I don't understand is why.

'I'm not staying here, I'll be the laughing stock of the village.'

She's right; I can see one or two women sniggering already. Tara sees them too and makes for the door. If looks could kill, Max would be dead on the floor by now. He doesn't try to stop her either but watches her walk past people with sympathetic faces. Faces that soon break into a smirk once out of her line of vision.

Max gets to his feet and faces me.

'How could you parody Tara like this? You know she has serious confidence issues.'

Do I? Max hasn't said anything to me.

'You know about her visits to her psychiatrist and how well she's been doing.'

Another no. What the hell is going on here? How would I possibly know any of these things?

'The house, the clothes and the other trappings of wealth are important to her, part of her recovery. She believes that stuff gives her an edge in this community. Tara needs to feel she's one of them, feel included. What you have done tonight will set her back months. I don't know what's going on inside that head of yours, Donna, but you'd better have a damn good explanation for your behaviour tonight.'

Am I living in some sort of alternate universe? Surely he remembers this afternoon and giving me the dress. As for the other stuff, Tara's mental state and all that, I had no idea.

'You gave me the damn dress to wear, the shoes, bag and even the pearls. Is this some sort of joke?'

He shakes his head and is now staring at the floor. He looks for all the world like a naughty child who's been caught out.

'The truth is, I've had a shit day, my head's in turmoil and right now I can barely remember my own name. I didn't mean for Tara to get so upset. It'll be a long time before she forgives either of us. Even worse, my Tara might never show her face in here again, which is a pity because it's a favourite of hers.'

My Tara... how dare he after what he's done. This has gone far enough; he's humiliated her, and me, come to that. Not that I give a toss about being made a show of. He might be angry but I'm quietly raging inside. I need to say something; Max can't walk away from this unscathed. I've seen another side to him tonight, a side that needs dealing with before his antics go beyond playing with his wife's emotions.

For three years I've done my best to stay out of trouble, to fend for myself and shrug off any attempt to wind me up, and I mean seriously wind me up. No drinking too much, no stealing food because I'm starving, and no run-ins with the law. If I'm left to get on with my life, everything is okay. These days I'm the peaceful type who doesn't court trouble.

But the other Donna is still here, bubbling away inside, just waiting for an opportunity to pounce. This Donna doesn't suffer with nerves, and she certainly doesn't have a conscience. This is bad Donna, and she's a world away from the Donna I'm trying to be now.

I am not the one in the wrong here and am not going to take the blame. I'm going to hand that back to the real culprit.

'You did this deliberately. You know exactly what you've done,' I say calmly. 'You set this up, sat back and watched your little pantomime play out.'

I'm not shouting but the restaurant has gone quiet as more and more people realise something is going on and turn to watch as Max and I face up to each other.

'You went to the trouble of buying another dress the exact same as the one Tara would wear. I trusted you, more fool me. I genuinely believed you wanted to help. For some twisted reason you wanted to create a scene tonight. From the look on Tara's face, you made a pretty good job of it. You're a louse, Max Marsden, and Tara won't let you get away with this. She'll make sure of that.'

He doesn't say a word for a few seconds, just stands there, arms folded and a pained expression on his face.

'Okay, I hold my hands up and I'll take the blame, but I really don't care for your tone towards me. Do you understand?'

'I'm sorry, but surely you understand the predicament. Tara is well known; this situation has hurt her in a way you can't imagine.'

He takes a step closer to me, a look of bewilderment on his face.

I'm having trouble believing that he could set up something like this and think it's okay.

'I don't like causing a scene, Donna. Right now we're the cabaret and it has to stop or people will talk. Apologise to me now, in front of these people, for causing a scene, or I will have to consider your position in my house.'

'It's Tara we should both apologise too. I'm happy to accept some of the blame for not checking with her first but you must talk to her, make her understand that you picked that dress out for me to wear tonight. If you don't want me to work for you, just say so. I'll be sorry, I like the job and what comes with it, but I won't stay where I'm not wanted.'

I wasn't aware until now that Hanna is stood right behind me. As I turn to leave, she claps her hands loudly and grins at me.

'You're a bloody star, Donna Slade. Well done for taking him on.'

FOURTEEN

I share a taxi back to the house with Hanna. She says nothing for the entire journey but sits next to me with a smile on her face.

As I enter the house, I hear weeping in the sitting room. I would try to comfort her but think better of it. I'm probably the last person Tara wants to see right now.

Max did this. I can take it, but I feel for poor Tara. What I can't work out is why he'd do such a thing. Is it a *man thing*, that he doesn't realise what he's done? I have to believe that. Anything else doesn't fit with the Max I'm getting to know.

I don't want to leave here either. He said he'd consider my position here. Fair enough, but I hope he sees sense and lets me stay. If not I'll never solve the mystery of Alice and that would torment me for the rest of my life.

'Please don't go,' a voice wails behind me. 'I won't get by without you.'

It's Hanna, upset and with tears running down her cheeks. Within the space of fifteen minutes her mood has completely changed. Where has the smug smile gone, the one she had on her face for the journey home?

'You were great back there, you stood up to him. You'll be alright now; he won't bother you again.'

'He didn't bother me tonight, Hanna. Everything he did was aimed at your mother. As for staying, that is up to your dad, you heard him. I'm afraid my future here is in the balance.'

'Where to, back to sofa surfing? You've got a home here, a good job and the other stuff you keep secret.'

'What are you talking about?' I hope it's not what I'm thinking.

'You know very well, Donna. You want to find out about Alice, who she was, where she came from. You won't be able to do that anywhere else but in this house.'

I'm shocked; it's as if she's read my mind. How does she know I'm looking into Alice? Did Alice tell her something, perhaps who she really was? If I have to leave here I give up any chance of finding out, of getting to the bottom of the Alice puzzle.

'I'll leave you to think things over. I don't want you to go. Life would be unbearable without you to share stuff with.'

With Hanna out of the way, I sit down on my bed to think. I have to talk to Max and make him change his mind. I hear another set of footsteps coming along the corridor and seconds later Max is stood in the doorway. Is my bedroom open house tonight? First Hanna, now Max has joined the party, no doubt with his big mouth and barmy ideas still in play.

'Have you come to gloat? You have caused chaos, upset your wife and practically sacked me – that's a great night's work, Max. You must be proud of yourself.'

Gone are the sexy smiles and the confident façade he presents to the world. This is a man who looks genuinely shocked and upset.

'I've no idea what came over me, Donna. I'm sorry for what happened tonight, for the pain I caused both you and Tara. Believe me when I tell you, I didn't do it on purpose. If I'd thought about it more carefully, remembered what dress I'd lent to you, things would have played out differently.'

'*Played*, Max! That was no game. What you did to Tara was upsetting; for a moment back there I thought this was you messing with her head. She was devastated when I walked into that restaurant.'

'I made a mistake; apart from my shit memory, I misheard something Tara told me about what she would wear. To be honest, I'm not interested in what she wears, Tara would look gorgeous in a sack.'

I have to agree; he's right there.

'That was some mistake, Max. You have a wife in tears who probably hates me now, and I've lost my job. All in all, a great night out,' I blast him.

'Give me a chance to explain.'

I look at him, arms folded, waiting for his excuse.

'Tara bought the blue dress from a boutique in the village. It was a little too small. That's the one I lent you. What I didn't know was that Tara had gone back and bought the same one in a larger size but didn't return the first one. It was a genuine mistake.'

That would be a reasonable excuse except for one thing. 'You and Tara travelled in the same taxi, surely you noticed what she was wearing?'

'I hold my hands up, you're right, and I'm sorry. But Tara wore a coat in the taxi and I didn't see what dress she had on underneath it. She was going on about wanting a holiday and, given the day I've had, I zoned out. All I remember about the ride there is her incessant chatter.'

I get that he didn't see the dress in the taxi, but he will have seen it when she took off the coat at the restaurant and sat at the table. Max's explanation doesn't hold water. But I must think carefully about what I say next. Despite my doubts about him, his face is a picture of remorse and guilt. Put on? I don't know him well enough to tell but it wouldn't surprise me. Max obviously likes to play games and I haven't got the energy for any of that. But if I walk out now, I'll be giving up the job and everything that goes with it. And then there's Alice. As much as I want to grab my stuff and run, I'd be stupid to do that.

'Okay, I accept your apology; what about my job?' He's said nothing about me keeping it so I have to ask.

'Of course the job is yours, Donna. Please stay.'

I give him a nod. 'Blame me for anything else I'm not responsible for and you won't be the only one considering my position here.'

I hope I've not made a mistake. Max has backtracked relatively easily, and I can't help feeling that I'm being manipulated.

'Fresh start then.' He smiles. 'I'll leave you in peace, I've still got to sort things with Tara.'

Good luck with that one, I think to myself.

Before he leaves the room, he walks to my side and kisses my cheek. I was not expecting that. I lean back, his eyes catch mine and linger for a few seconds longer than they should. I'm thinking like a smitten teenager again. For the sake of my own sanity this has to stop.

FIFTEEN

It's one in and one out in my little sitting room tonight as the moment Max leaves, Hanna is back and with a smile on her face. She's obviously been listening.

'Happier now?' I ask her.

'You've no idea how glad I am that you're not leaving but you must be careful,' she warns. 'He gave in too easily, and apologising is way out of character.'

'I will be on my guard, don't worry about that. All I ask from him is to be left alone to get on with the work.'

'And the other thing, the Alice mystery.'

'Can we talk about that tomorrow? I'm tired and I have a headache from what happened tonight. I just haven't the energy.'

'Okay, I'll see you in the morning.'

I've had enough of tonight. Thrashing things out with Max has helped but there are still questions, and while she's here, Hanna can answer at least one of them.

'When we arrived at the restaurant, you didn't come inside with me, you wanted me to go it alone; why was that?'

She turns her face from me, shaking her head.

'If I tell you, promise you won't hate me.'

'If you've anything to say then spit it out.'

'Max told me to make sure you entered the restaurant on your own,' is her simple answer. 'I had no idea what he had planned, but if I want a quiet life I do as I'm told.'

He didn't want Hanna distracting attention from me. He wanted to make sure that Tara got the full impact. Max knew exactly what he was doing tonight, it had nothing to do with a faulty memory as he wanted me to believe. Both me and Tara are the victims tonight; I hope she gives him hell.

'It's okay, Hanna, I do understand. If he bullies you like that again, tell me.'

She gives me a weak smile and watches me unpack the stuff I'd shoved into my sports bag.

'You do know that Max doesn't want us to be friends,' she tells me.

'Why on earth not?'

I think Hanna is exaggerating there. I can't see any reason why Max would want that.

'Max has a lot to hide. He's afraid that I'll tell you things. Things that could harm him.'

As tired as I am I can't go to bed wondering what she means by that. I'll just lie awake all night thinking about it. 'Go on then, tell me more.'

'I daren't. You let something slip and, if Max finds out, I'll be punished.'

After tonight I know she's not lying. I look at her and shake my head.

'*Punished*,' I echo. 'If he even dares, you make sure to tell me straight away. I dealt with him tonight and I can do it again,' I assure her. 'Don't worry; you don't have to tell me anything until you're ready.'

I only hope I can keep my curiosity in check. As for Max, I can't keep up with the behaviour changes; one minute he's fine and the next he's almost dangerous. I don't know whether to like him or hate him. 'You've stood outside my old bedroom, you must wonder why I don't use it anymore and sleep next door. I daren't sleep in there, it scares me too much. It's proof of how much Max hates me, and I'm too ashamed to take you or anyone else in there.'

I'm clueless; what can possibly be in there that Hanna is ashamed of?

'Max is clever. Every punishment, every go he has at upsetting me, is psychological. He's never laid a finger on me. His way of punishing people is more subtle than that.'

'Want to tell me?'

Her face clouds over as she looks at me with those piercing eyes. I want to help her but unless she opens up there's nothing I can do.

'Perhaps I'll tell you one day but not now,' is the answer I get. 'You are more at risk than me. The more you find out about Max, the more danger you're in. He'll be watching you from now on. Apart from Alice, you're the only person who's ever taken him on. I worry that something will happen to you like it did to her.'

My heart races as I take in what she's just said. 'You said Alice's death was an accident?'

'It's what Max told the police at the time, and they were happy with that, but neither me nor Tara saw it happen, so we don't know for sure. We know only what Max told us.'

'You're overthinking it, Hanna. An accident is just that. There's no need to get paranoid about it.'

She doesn't look convinced.

'You will be careful though, won't you? He's sly and doesn't like to lose. You got the better of him tonight and that will make him even more determined to get even.'

'I can look after myself, Hanna. You mustn't worry.'

I hadn't spent most of the last three years living in grimy old bedsits, getting into fights with drunk neighbours and going without food, and not learned a thing or two. Accepting the offer of a job has given Max the opportunity to mess with someone else's head other than Tara's, but I've got something out of it too: the chance to sort out the Alice problem. No more distractions, from now on that has to be my number one priority. I cannot allow this family to get in the way.

'If I do stay here, do you promise to help me find out about Alice?'

'You wouldn't run away? Please promise me you won't just disappear. Stay and I'll help you with anything I can.'

The look on her face tells me she means it. She needs me but I want something in return. I'm not proud of myself for doing this but I will use Hanna's reliance on me to get what I want.

'You want help with the name thing, don't you? You want to know why Alice or whoever she was stole yours.'

I'm stunned and can't speak; I want to ask how she knows that but the words won't come. Hanna is staring at me, she knows very well what's going on in my head. Turmoil about sums it up. One thing I'm sure of, she didn't just pluck that out of thin air; someone must have told her. It can only have been Alice herself. Alice knew the young woman far better than I do and must have known that Hanna can't be trusted, so why tell her?

SIXTEEN

'I know what you're thinking, Donna.' Hanna smirks at me. 'You're wondering how I know about you. It's dead simple: Alice, or whoever she was, said that Alice wasn't her name and that one day soon the real Alice would turn up.'

Alice could not have known that; I didn't know myself until a week ago.

'Did she tell you why she used another name?'

'No, she told me that she had to borrow the name to protect herself. She also said that when you came here, you'd use the name Donna.'

How did she know? Alice, a woman I've never met, not only knew my real name but also the one I buried under layers of secrecy, the one I thought was safe. That should be impossible, unless she has been keeping tabs on me.

I fight back the need to throw up. This is a nightmare and I don't know what to do. Alice came to this house for a reason; was I lured here for the same one? Did she tell anyone about me? Is someone else going to turn up? If that happens, how do I react?

I want to know why Alice thought she needed protection.

Does that mean I'm in danger too? Like me she must have wanted to disappear for a good reason. My head is brimming with questions but I doubt Hanna will be able to answer them all.

'When you first came here I thought you must know the truth about Alice, that's why you were at her funeral.'

Shaking my head, I reply, 'I was invited by email, that's why I came. You and Alice talked a lot about things. Are you sure she didn't give you my email address and it was you who sent the invite to me?' It would make things simpler if that's what happened; otherwise I'm knee-deep in a big problem. Someone else I've never met knows more about me than they should.

'I promise you, Donna, it wasn't me. Alice mentioned your name a couple of times but that was all.'

'Attending Alice's funeral, seeing my name on that coffin, was a terrifying experience. I'd no idea what was going on. I've only stayed here in the hope I can find the truth. If you know anything at all, Hanna, you have to tell me.'

'I'll help you all I can, but Alice told me precious little about her life before she came here or her family. I've no idea who she was. I've thought about that a lot. I reckon she must have been someone you knew. Otherwise it doesn't make any sense.'

Hanna smiles at me. 'I know it's not your real name, but you don't mind if I still call you Donna.'

I don't mind at all. If she calls me Alice, her parents will start with the questions.

'Donna is fine. I can't imagine your parents being happy if they find out I've been lying to them, and they certainly won't be pleased that you knew and kept it to yourself either.'

'I won't tell anyone, I promise. You can trust me on that.'

'We'll speak tomorrow, Hanna.' I yawn again.

'I'll leave you in peace, see you at breakfast.'

Finally I'm on my own, just me and dozens of questions. Sleep will be impossible for a while. I can hear Max and Tara arguing downstairs, and that won't help either. Max's voice is dominant, I imagine he can be heard throughout the house. He's giving her hell about what happened with the dress. Tara is trying to fight back but losing. Poor Tara, she's no match for Max.

I hear Tara scream Hanna's name. I'm not being nosey but I want to know what is being said. I don't want the pair blaming her for any of it. I creep onto the landing, intending to stand and listen at the top of the staircase. But I immediately change my mind when I see what's lying on the floor.

The blue dress, the one Tara wore, is lying in tatters, the pieces strewn on the carpet outside my door. Someone is trying to tell me something. A message, perhaps a warning, but why? Hanna has only just left me, Max is downstairs laying into Tara, which begs the question, who did this?

What have I got myself into?

SEVENTEEN

The next morning, the last thing I want to do is face Max and Tara in the office. I'm praying Tara leaves the topic of the dress alone or, if not, that she lays the blame at Max's feet where it belongs. He is responsible, regardless of any excuse he will have spouted to her.

I don't feel too good either; I have to crawl out of bed. My reflection in the mirror is very different from last night. My face is pale, I've got dark circles under my eyes and my hair has developed a life of its own. I'm fit for nothing but falling back into bed and sleeping the day away.

That's not possible, I'm afraid. Me appearing in the office today is a must. I won't give Max the satisfaction of thinking I haven't shown up because of him. If Tara plays the blame game, I'll have to deal with it as best I can. The woman isn't stupid; she knows full well what her husband's like.

Taking a deep breath, I leave my rooms, lock the door behind me and start down the corridor towards the office. On the way, I pass Maria, the housekeeper. She says nothing but I hear her laughing under her breath. Does she know about last night? I reckon she does, and that will be down to Max. Perhaps they even had a laugh at my expense. We haven't even been introduced and already she's treating me like a figure of fun. Any more piss-taking and I'll blow. There's just so much I'm prepared to stand.

I've no sooner sat at my desk when Max bursts into my office and smiles at me as if we're best friends. I wish he'd turn it off, I'm not in the mood, and after a crap night's sleep I'm certainly not impressed.

'I'm sorry about last night,' he says. 'Tara is the real villain in this. She chose to wear the dress deliberately because she knew I'd lent you the other one.'

Not what he told me last night. Take him on yet again or let it go… I need a couple of painkillers before I decide.

'I only wanted to help. To make sure you felt confident and had a good time. I've sung your praises once too often and this is Tara's reaction. She's at an age where she is jealous of women who are younger than her. It isn't that she dislikes them, more she sees them as rivals. Sabotaging the evening was her way of getting back at both you and me. I should have known, read the signs, but I didn't. When Tara gets like this she can't help herself.'

He is joking. Tara had nothing to do with this, and all this bullshit about me is a blatant attempt at getting me onside. Does he not remember the chat we had late last night or the stand-off between us in front of all those people in the restaurant? Obviously not; he's still playing some sort of game. Either way, I want to keep my job for now, so time to throw a smile of my own into the ring.

'Don't worry, Max, I understand. I'm prepared to forget what happened last night and just get on with my job.'

Definitely not true, but complaining, calling him a barefaced liar, will make things worse, so not a good idea. Right now I fancy the quiet life and a peaceful day. I also need time to tease out of Hanna all the information she can give me on Alice. That won't happen if I stir things up with her dad.

'Look, I know you haven't been with us for very long, but you'll soon see that Tara is delicate and very vulnerable.'

Here we go, he is going to play the 'she has problems, has to take pills for her nerves' card again.

'She is recovering from a particularly bad bout of depression.'

Living with you will do that, is what I want to throw back at him but I hold my tongue.

'Last night is typical behaviour since she's been feeling down. Tara is insanely jealous of any woman who I show any interest in. I half expected something like this. Embarrassing people is one thing but what she's really after is sympathy, to get people onside, turn them against me.'

I don't believe a word of it but I give him a smile and begin to rifle through the in-tray on my desk.

'You must have seen what she did to Hanna's bedroom,' he continues. 'She will have told you the décor, the furniture and that awful graffiti are down to me. That isn't true. Tara poisoned Hanna's mind on that one. The truth: Tara is responsible for all of it. It was after that incident that Tara spent time in hospital.'

Hanna's bedroom? Everything looked okay to me when she invited me in to look at that grey dress. Max must be talking about the room next door, the one Hanna keeps locked.

'Tara thinks everyone is against her. It's nothing new; it started when she was young. Tara's parents told me she destroyed her toys then told her teachers they had done it. I was aware of this when I married her. I stupidly thought that I could change her, make her happy and content. It seems to me that things are slipping again.'

He'd make a damn good actor. He looks close to tears, very much like a man who isn't lying through his teeth.

'I had to explain things to you, Donna. I'm not a danger to

you but you will have to watch your step where Tara is concerned. She has a fixation with Isabel, a friend of ours. You'll remember her from the funeral, one of the two women stood behind us.'

The woman hurling insults, of course I remember her, stuck-up cow. Max certainly has his faults but to take her as his mistress when he's married to the lovely Tara is beyond belief.

'Tara's convinced herself that me and Isabel are having an affair. Totally wrong of course but no amount of denial will convince her. She's even hoodwinked Hanna into believing the lie. Hanna will tell you things about me, how I treat her badly. That isn't true. She's our only child. All I want to do is take care of her, spoil her, but she doesn't even call us Mum and Dad, for heaven's sake.'

Isabel is all in Tara's mind, Hanna's too, if Max is to be believed. 'I'm sorry, you have a lot to cope with.' I do my best to sound sincere. He tells me fairy stories, I appear to accept them, and that way I'll get the quiet life I'm after.

'Anything you're concerned about, Donna, if Tara starts on you again, come and tell me. Better I have a word than you get upset. I want you to stay with us, you're just what this office needs.'

I can't believe I'm that important to have around but it's a con. I'm not so stupid that I believe him.

Another smile and a nod of my head. I am so two-faced at times I even impress myself.

'I'm pleased we've cleared the air but it's about time we got on with the day.'

He passes me a wodge of papers.

'After filing those, Donna, get the latest outgoings from the spreadsheet to Tara. I can't imagine why but she's fussing about profit again.'

Neither can I. Max's business is phenomenally profitable. I've already gone over the accounts and the spreadsheets in an effort to get a grip on them. From what I've seen there's nothing to worry about.

Given that Max is in a better mood and eager to please, dare I ask him about Alice, get him talking about the accident? I decide not; off-the-cuff questions won't do. I must think carefully, make them sound like natural curiosity and not something important to me.

He said I was attractive. Two days ago, even yesterday, I'd have been over the moon, but not this morning. I didn't sleep last night but I did weigh everything up, Max included. I can't believe I had a *thing* for him. Imagine what Hanna would do with that one. She'd call me stupid, and she'd be right. She certainly wouldn't trust me.

Ten minutes later, I have a printout of the figures ready for Tara. A short walk up the corridor and a quick peep through the glass window of Max's office, and I see her sat at his desk. I tap, she sees me and comes to get the printouts. Not a smile in sight.

'I've not forgiven you, so don't ask. I hate people taking my things without permission. That dress is a favourite of mine and I have no idea why you went through my wardrobe.'

The woman has two of them, for goodness' sake. Hasn't Max spoken to her, explained what happened? From what she'd just said and the look on her face, I reckon not. The mood she's in, telling her my wearing the dress was down to Max or that he's already spoken to me is a waste of time. She's dead set on pinning the blame for last night on me, and that's that.

'Sorry, it won't happen again.' I decide that simple and to the point is best. I haven't got the energy for a lengthy row.

'Make sure it doesn't, or you'll suffer the consequences.'

Was she threatening me? I don't question it as it won't do to rile her further. She might persuade Max to sack me. I don't think Max would go for that, not after what he said to me earlier, but you never know.

Minutes after I'd returned to my desk, Tara's in my face again. What is it this time?

'I know it was you,' she accuses me. 'There isn't anyone else it could have been.'

The dress, I wonder. Hadn't she said enough already? 'I thought we'd sorted that problem so what d'you think I've done now?' My voice is brittle, unamused, exactly how I feel.

'This isn't about the dress.'

Tara folds her arms, her eyes blaze at me. I've no idea what she's talking about. I shake my head and look her in the eyes, my expression just as angry as hers.

'An eighteen-carat gold necklace is missing from the jewellery box on my dressing table. It has a large emerald drop with a filigree surround. It can only be you who took it, no one else would dare. If I don't find it, I'll have no choice but to call the police. I don't want to do that, Donna. I'm giving you a chance to put this right, but this is your first and last opportunity to apologise and give it back.'

The words fall out of her mouth so fast I can barely keep up. She stares at me with a look I've not seen before. A mixture of regret and disappointment.

Speed talk over, I've finally got the gist.

'It wasn't me. I'd never steal from you.' All brittleness is gone from my voice as I try to be calm and truthful. Not easy or always successful. Put on the spot, my hands shake and my voice goes up an octave. It's easy to see why she doesn't believe me. When I'm accused of anything, I automatically feel guilty even though I'm not.

'This isn't what I expect from you. We offered you a new start, a new job and this is how you repay us? We have to trust you. I don't want to ask you to leave but if you don't give me the necklace back, I'll have no choice.

Tara didn't make her point quietly. Max must have heard

the noise from downstairs, and within seconds he bounded up to join us.

'What's all the noise about? I'm trying to go through contracts down there.'

Tara is standing only inches away from me, hands on hips and looking ready to pounce. Before the situation gets worse, Max drags Tara away from my desk.

His eyes fix firmly on Tara. 'Is one of you going to tell me what the hell is going on?'

'She's stolen my emerald necklace, the one you bought me for our anniversary. After the incident with the dress, no one else would have the nerve, so she's the only suspect.'

Nice, and there was me thinking all this nonsense was finished.

Max shakes his head in dismay, reaches into the pocket of his trousers and pulls out what has to be the very necklace. I heave a sigh of relief but Tara's face pales.

'I've got it. Remember you told me the fastener was broken and you were afraid it would slip off your neck?'

Her anger is gone to be replaced by wide eyes and a quivering lip. Will she apologise for her mistake? No such luck; saying sorry must be beneath her. Ignoring me, she clings onto Max while he wipes the tears from her eyes. Put on? It wouldn't surprise me. What does surprise me though is the way Tara flew at me. Max can't have acted on our conversation earlier. Putting that aside for the moment, I'm grateful that Max has saved the day, not to mention my bacon. He knows how to handle Tara in a strop, a talent I can do with acquiring.

There's no apology, not even a second look, as Max leads Tara away with his arm around her waist. Within minutes, Hanna's in my face again.

'He's keeping her sweet. That's why all the pretence, stepping in and saving the day. No way was he having the necklace fixed. He'll have taken it himself to piss Tara off.'

'That's devious, but it shouldn't surprise me. I believe that man is capable of anything.'

'He's a smooth operator, gives people the impression that he's kind, and generous, but you and I both know that he's a rogue. Tara is easily fooled and that does my head in.'

Tara might be difficult to live with but I doubt Max would fool his own wife about a necklace like this. But perhaps that wasn't what he was doing at all. It was me that got it in the neck. If Max hadn't produced the thing, Tara might have called the police. If he is operating a nudge on the wrong side of the law, that would have opened a can of worms. I suppose that, whatever the reason, he did step in and save me from the wrath of Tara. Perhaps I'm supposed to be grateful to him. He hasn't got a hope in hell.

'*Keeping her sweet*, you said... what did you mean by that?'

'The necklace goes missing. Tara blames you. Max produces it, making its disappearance from her jewellery box a non-event. That throws Tara off balance emotionally.'

'Why would he do that?'

'He's seeing Isabel tonight.'

Isabel, the mistress. Not fifteen minutes ago he told me that was simply Tara's imagination playing up. I feel a sudden sympathy for Tara. Whatever the relationship is between her and Max, she doesn't deserve this. Max is deliberately playing on her psychological weaknesses.

'Tara knows about Isabel but she and Max have never spoken about her. Having things out in the open is not a good look as far as Max is concerned. He has to hang on to Tara; he wants the business world to believe that he and she are the perfect partnership. Compromise that and it will have consequences. The people he deals with like and respect her. Tara is vital to the smooth running of the business.'

'Have you any idea how Isabel feels about his reliance on Tara?'

'Pissed off, I imagine, but Isabel will get hers one of these days. Nothing lasts for ever, and that includes her relationship with Max. Tara won't acknowledge the affair. She'd rather pretend it isn't happening. That way there's no arguing, and Max has the best of both worlds.'

What a way to live. I'm not surprised Tara needs pills to stay sane; stay here for much longer and I'll need them too.

'You will have seen her at the funeral. Black hair, bright-red lipstick and a loud mouth she thinks everyone wants to hear from.'

'Would Max ever leave Tara?'

'He might be into Isabel now but, like I say, it won't last. Give it a few months and he'll ditch her for someone else. Tara will find out, do nothing, and so it starts again. He knows all the moves too. After the spat they just had, Tara is after Max's sympathy; she'll get it too. He'll give her some pill or other and she'll sleep until tomorrow. Leaving Max with the whole night to play with.

This is one dysfunctional family. The best thing to do for the time being is to keep my head down. Don't know anything, don't see anything and don't have an opinion. That way I can get on with what I'm here for and not become embroiled in family arguments.

EIGHTEEN

It's five the next morning when I hear the front door open and close. The alarm hasn't gone off so it has to be one of the family. Max is the obvious candidate. If Hanna is right, he must have been out galivanting with this Isabel all night. I know Max is a louse but I'm still surprised at his behaviour. Tara is beautiful; she helps with his business and runs this house. Isabel isn't a patch on her, particularly in the looks department.

As much as I'd like to help Tara, I daren't. 'Don't get involved' is what I'd decided, and I intend to stick to that plan. I have more pressing problems anyway.

The Alice Anderson who'd worked here had a name of her own. She certainly wasn't me, so why the impersonation? I need to know more about her, and my best bet is Hanna. At lunchtime I'll seek her out, ask a few questions, get her talking.

I spend the morning dealing with the accounts, and sending emails for Max. He's in a good mood and relaxed, because he'd seen Isabel the night before or because Tara is having a lie in and out of the way? Whichever, it's no concern of mine. I have work to do and I want to get my next conversation with Hanna straight in my mind.

From my office window I can see Hanna hard at it. She's working with Max's pigs. Feeding and cleaning them out, I imagine. A thankless task – poor girl, I don't envy her. It's not something I could do. At lunchtime I'll make us both a couple of sandwiches and join her. I want to get her talking about Alice. I need something to work with, no matter how small.

Maria is busy preparing lunch when I walk into the kitchen. Despite the snigger she'd given me earlier, I smile and politely ask if I might make a quick bite for me and Hanna. All I get back is a nod, no words. No sign of friendliness at all. Ignoring her, I get on with it. In the fridge I find a pack of ham, nice and quick. I butter the bread and layer the ham onto it. I grab a couple of cans of soft drinks and am about to go outside to find Hanna when Maria calls to me.

'Are you liking it here?'

I'm surprised she asks; up until now she's ignored me.

'Yes, I think so. Have you worked here long?'

'Two years,' she answers. 'But unlike you I don't like it here at all.'

I want to ask her why, but she turns from me, grabs the rubbish bin and walks away. I've got an hour for lunch and want to see Hanna, speaking to Maria is one for the back burner.

As I walk towards Hanna, she spots the food in my hands and gives me a wide grin for my trouble.

'At last.' She nods as I approach. 'No one ever thinks about how tough this job is and how hungry I get doing it.'

She's wearing overalls and wipes the palms of her hands down the sides before taking the sandwiches from me.

'Aw, well I'm glad to be the first one to think of you,' I say with a smile. 'A girl working as hard as you needs sustenance.'

'Thanks, I appreciate it.'

Looking around at the pig pen, I cringe. No way could I tackle what Hanna is doing. In the pen there are at least a dozen full-grown pigs, every one of them with their snouts rooting in the mud. Hanna sees the distasteful look on my face and shakes her head.

'I don't do this out of choice, you know? Max makes me,' she says. 'He knows I'm terrified of the filthy things, that being so close to them freaks me out, but he doesn't care. He thinks it's highly amusing to see me up to my eyes in mud and pig shit.'

'You've told him how you feel?'

'Makes no difference. He's convinced Tara that it's good for me to get involved, and that the exercise will help me lose weight.'

'Have you tried putting Tara right?'

'She knows well enough but she does what Max says. He insists I do the job, so she agrees. He enjoys seeing me suffer. The man's not right in the head. There are times when I think the pigs mean more to him than we do. I do it because I need him to finance my business venture; otherwise I wouldn't bother.

Personally, I doubt Max will ever give Hanna the money she needs. Why would he? She leaves home and he's left with only Tara to torment.

She points at one of the piglets begging for her sandwich. Throwing it a crust, she says, 'The piglets are cute though. It's a shame they grow into such ugly creatures.'

'Looking after them must be hard?'

'Mucking out is. The mess they make stinks and it's damned hard to shift. Feeding them is okay. They eat all the waste food from the kitchen; nothing gets thrown away. They're greedy too, always on the hunt for something to eat, and they're not fussy. They're supposed to be fed on food made specially for them, but we don't stick to that. Max says why should we? They'll eat anything and are happy enough, even the piglets.'

She snaps open the can of soft drink and takes a swig.

'Alice,' I begin. 'Do you know her real name?'

'I don't know very much about her. She was secretive, didn't discuss her past and didn't make any friends locally while she was with us.'

'Did she ever slip up, tell you something that seemed odd at the time?'

'I know Alice Anderson wasn't her real name,' she says with a smirk.

We both know that's old news.

'No, the problem with Alice was she kept most of the chat about Max's business; regarding that she was seriously vocal. She was continually pointing out weaknesses in the procedures they use. The accounts were a case in point. It was Alice who got Max to buy the new accounts package. She was amazed that a company with such a large turnover was still using hand-written ledgers.'

'Did your parents ever question her identity?'

'She fooled them along with everyone else. Alice was brilliant at acting a part. In fact, she was brilliant at most things. She was the perfect PA, learned her lines well, and there wasn't anything about Max's business she didn't know.'

I've had my own run-in with Max. Is it possible that Alice did find out something about the business that Max wanted kept secret? Could he have engineered her death or am I simply letting my imagination run wild again? Possibly, but I'm going to keep that thought in mind.

'Come on, Hanna. I think you know a lot more about Alice than you're saying, and I'm not sure why you're not sharing it with me. You know that Alice wasn't her real name for a start, how come?'

'Okay, you're right,' she says, surprising me. 'I do know a bit more about her. We got a letter one day addressed to Nancy Williams, care of Alice Anderson. Weird having two names on it but Alice didn't think so. I was bothered about the other name but Alice wasn't and insisted that she would deal with it, give it to this Nancy woman.'

Nancy Williams is a name I know only too well. She is a woman dear to me, the only woman I ever trusted. Hearing it on Hanna's lips makes me go cold. Now the questions are boundless. Why would someone write to her and send the letter to Alice? The only reason I can think of is that the Alice that this family knew was Nancy. If I'm right, why did she masquerade as me? She must have come here with a purpose; it can't have happened by chance.

One thought does cross my mind: if Alice was Nancy, then whoever sent the letter knew this and was looking for me. That isn't something I'm comfortable with; it means someone out there knows where Alice was living.

If I understand things right, it also means that the only woman who genuinely cared for me as a child is dead from a stupid accident. I have to find out if that fall down the stairs was as I've been told or something more sinister.

NINETEEN

I'm momentarily struck dumb but don't want Hanna to cotton on that the name has had any effect on me.

'Did your parents ask Alice about the letter?' finally falls out of my mouth while crossing my fingers that the answer is *no*.

'The post is delivered early in the morning so my parents didn't see the letter on the mat, but I did.'

'Did Alice tell you anything about this Nancy?'

'Alice was a good friend to me, she helped me cope with Max, but she had secrets. I asked about the letter many times, but she refused to tell me if she'd passed it on to Nancy or not. She wouldn't tell me who the woman was either. A few days after the letter arrived, she went off sick for a week, not like her at all. Pissed Max off big style, that did.'

I have no doubt now that the woman who came here and used my name was in fact Nancy Williams. I can think of any number of people who might write to her, but whoever sent the letter had to know where she was. I'm having difficulty working out who Nancy would trust with the information. I'll work on that one later; for now I'll settle for knowing if Hanna read it.

'Do you know anything about the letter, like who sent it or what was in it?'

'I asked her more than once but she insisted that she hadn't opened it and that she intended to pass it on. She told me not to tell my parents about it either as they'd only ask questions. It was all very strange. I told her if she didn't know where this Nancy was, she should give it back to the postman, but Alice said she wanted to keep it until she met up with Nancy. She told me that she had somewhere special to hide it where it wouldn't be found.'

If I'm right, I know exactly where that is.

'Someone must have cleared her stuff out after she died. Was the letter found?'

'Me and Tara did that, but no letter. We sent a lot of her stuff to the charity shop in the village, and they were pleased to have it; Alice had some nice clothes. I checked all the pockets thoroughly and made sure her handbags were empty but found nothing. She must have passed it on after all.'

She kept it, I'm sure of that.

'What about Max, do you think he could have taken it?'

'Even if he knew she'd got a letter, I can't see him being that interested. As far as I know, he didn't really care about Alice or whatever she was up to.'

'What did Alice bring with her? Did she have any knick-knacks, ornaments she was fond of?'

'She had some of those glass things that you have, little animals and birds. She used to dot them on surfaces around her rooms. She had dozens, even more than Max's china pigs.'

I have seen Max's ornaments. There is an entire cabinet full of them in a corner of the sitting room.

'Then there was an old-fashioned box she was fond of, a wooden thing about the size of a biscuit tin with carvings of animals all around it. Alice told me it had belonged to her grandfather.'

'That went to charity as well?'

Hanna nods. 'Old as it is, no one's bought it yet. I saw it earlier on in the week in the charity shop window.'

Alice or Nancy having the box confirms her identity. This is a breakthrough, a question I can tick off the list. I've seen the box Hanna just described before, many years ago, as a child. I know it has a secret drawer, the perfect place to hide a letter.

'I want that box, Hanna. I'll nip out later and see if it's still there.'

'Why are you so interested, Donna? It looked like a dirty old thing to me.'

'I reckon the letter is inside it.'

'What makes you think that?'

'I think I know who Alice really was, and that's exactly where she'd hide it.'

'You don't *think*; you *know*. I can see it on your face. You know exactly who she is.'

I struggle to hide my emotions at times and this is one of them. Nancy is the only person from my old life who I've missed since I left home. She was kind, generous and affectionate. She tried hard to make things right for me, make my mother take responsibility, a thankless task. I did try to find her in the early days when I first left home but had no success. A neighbour from the same street where we used to live told me that she'd moved away. The thought of reading a letter that she wrote has brought a lump to my throat.

'I can get it for you,' Hanna suggests. 'You don't know the village, not even how to get there.'

'Don't worry, it's only down the road, I'll find it.'

Nice of her to offer but I don't want Hanna involved if I can help it. Her mood fluctuates; she can be helpful and likeable, but her mood can flip and she's the opposite. Someone sent that letter and I want to know who and why. To use my name and disappear from her usual life, I reckon Nancy was frightened of someone, and that letter might tell me who.

'You believe Alice is really Nancy Williams, don't you? You recognised the name when I first said it.'

'It's a possibility,' I lie.

I don't want to tell Hanna just yet but I'm certain that Alice is Nancy. It was the box that did it. Old and battered it might be, but Nancy treasured it. There's no way she'd have given it away to someone else or lose it.

'I don't think Max will give you time off, not even an hour to nip into the village, and the shop closes early today. Even if he does, he'll want to know where you're going and why.'

She has a point. I've no idea if I'm out of favour or not so it's not worth asking; he'd be curious and I don't want the interrogation. But I don't want to leave it until the weekend either, the box could have been sold by then. Looks like it's down to Hanna after all.

'If it's still there I can get it for you this afternoon. I'll pay and you can owe me the money.'

Despite my reservations it's kind of her to offer, and it would solve my problem, providing she hands it over, that is.

'I'll repay you out of my first wage.'

'I'm glad to help. I'm as curious about Alice as you are. I'll tell you this much, I guessed Alice was a fraud right from the start. Don't ask me why, it was an instinct sort of thing. As far as I'm concerned, that letter was a giveaway. I asked her about it, asked why she was so keen to keep hold of the thing. She said I'd got it all wrong, but I hadn't. She was Nancy Williams, and no amount of denying it was going to work with me.'

I need to take the heat out of this. I'll have to think of something else Hanna can get her teeth into. My mystery is becoming the centre of her life.

'You don't know for sure, Hanna. It was only one letter, it's no big deal.'

Hanna shook her head. 'Alice recognised the name, took the letter, kept it and didn't speak about it again. I'll tell you something else, that letter did her no good at all.'

I want to drop this now. I have to get back to the office or Max will be on the warpath.

'I've got to go, work to do.' It's the truth, there's a pile of paperwork waiting on my desk.

'But I am enjoying our little chat.' She looks at me like a spoilt child. 'Stay a bit longer, I might remember more about that letter and what Alice said.'

I'm losing patience. 'If you know something, Hanna, then spit it out. I'd like to chat the day away too, but that's not how it works. I've got work to do and I don't want your father on my back.'

'It's always the same, you only give me the time of day when you want something. You're as bad as the rest of them, it's all self, self, self.'

'That's not true. You know how I'm fixed, I'm here to work.'

'Work, that's a laugh; you spend all your time on the Alice thing. What if I tell Max, d'you think he'd be so keen to keep you here then?'

'You won't do that.'

'I might, and if I do, you will never know the truth.'

She is pissing me off now. 'The truth, Hanna? You mean your truth, and I'm not sure I trust that.'

'Well, you should. I haven't lied to you yet.'

She gives me that sneaky smile, the one I dislike. What's coming now, some revelation she's deliberately kept from me?

'You know Max paid for the funeral, and it wasn't cheap. Not because he was fond of Alice; that's a load of rubbish. He paid out of guilt.'

'Come on, Hanna, what has he to feel guilty about?'

'There you go again, missing what's in front of you because

you think you know him better than me. Well, you don't. Max is a two-timing, manipulative man who wants his own way.'

'I've heard enough, go and waste someone else's time.'

'You need to hear me out, before you make the same mistakes as Alice.'

'Go away, Hanna.'

'You'll be sorry, he'll come after you like he did with her.'

This is getting silly now.

'You need to be careful, watch your back.'

Hanna is good at dishing out the drama but I'm not in the mood. 'You make it sound as if Max is dangerous.'

'He is, idiot,' she practically screams at me. 'I think he killed Alice.'

TWENTY

My heart pounds as I realise that this isn't one of Hanna's fantasies. She looks scared. I have already considered that Alice's death might not have been a natural one. The official line is that she tumbled down the stairs and hit her head on the newel post at the bottom. Certainly possible, but it does leave plenty of room for speculation.

'Do you have any evidence that Max was involved? Where was he when it happened?'

'He was upstairs too; I heard him talking on the phone. He must have heard her scream and appeared at the top of the landing before Alice had even reached the bottom. He rushed down after her, but it was too late.'

'You told me Max was out at the time; which is it, Hanna?'

'I get confused, but thinking about it, he was definitely here. He was first on the scene when she fell. It was a traumatic experience. Is it any wonder I don't remember it exactly?'

'Do you remember any clearer now?'

'Yes I do; I was in the hall and heard the sickening thud as her head hit that post.'

He was there. More than that, he was close enough to have pushed her. Does Max have it in him to murder someone? I've only known him a short time, but it is possible that Hanna could be right; the man is unpredictable, the incident with the dress told me that. But if Max did push her, that begs the question *why*.

I regret coming here, meeting these people and getting myself involved in something so dangerous. But I have to find out who sent me the invite, because whoever it was knows exactly who I really am, and indeed who Nancy was too... and if they tracked me down once, they could do that again, even if I run... unless I find them, but first I have to find out who they are.'

I'm on my way back to the office when I realise that I've forgotten all about the data stick; mind you, given everything that's happened, I'm not surprised. It must have been Nancy who hid it, and she must have had a reason. Why else would she put my name on it?

Back in the office, Max has left a note on my desk. He wants printouts of all the emails received this week. Easy enough and shouldn't take long.

Two hours later, after sorting the printouts and having had a good look through the filing cabinets, it's time to call it a day. There's nothing in them of any interest, just boring stuff like buyer's details. I'll hand the printouts to either Max or Tara and then it's back to the memory stick.

Max isn't in his office. I know I'm not supposed to enter but I want the printouts off my hands. I would leave them on his desk but as usual the door's locked. I've no choice but to wander round the house in search of Tara. I've not seen Hanna for hours either and have no idea if she managed to buy the box or not. I could do without the hassle of chasing that one up. It's late; all I want is for her to hand the box over, an hour on my laptop and then it's straight to bed.

I'm halfway down the stairs when the front doorbell rings. I've been here a few days now and not once has anyone come to the house. I don't know why that is; they must have friends and relatives, so why no visitors?

When Max answers the door, I hear the voice and know that it's Nicco, the man I met at the wake. The pair are arguing loudly and I hear Max's raised voice, so I decide to give them a wide berth and not to interrupt the argument. Whatever the problem is between them, the row is getting more heated by the second, and I can't help but be intrigued by what could cause such upset. I want to hear what the pair are arguing about so I watch from behind the staircase spindles, praying that neither of them spots me.

I thought Nicco a nice man when I first met him; he was kind to me and I won't forget that he was one of very few people who gave me a warm welcome that day.

I listen to him now and he couldn't be more different to the man I met; he's very angry about something and he keeps smacking one fist into the other. Given his size, he could flatten Max at any time. I want to help Max but that's a ridiculous idea. My five-foot-nothing frame against that huge man is laughable. Even if Max and I both took him on, he's so big we'd get nowhere. The best thing to do is retreat back up the stairs and hunker down but I'm glued to the spot, watching what's happening. I want to know why Nicco is in such a bad temper. Nosey of me, I know, but I could learn something useful.

Although I have spoken to Nicco, I have no idea if he is connected to Max's business or not, but they aren't talking houses or money. There is no missing Nicco's voice; he's shouting the name Isabel and threatening Max with his fists. I hear Max tell him that he'll sort it, whatever *it* is. Even from this distance I can see that doesn't impress Nicco.'

'I've heard it all before, Max, but it's still going on. I should be your accountant, not her. You only took her on because you're sleeping with her. If it comes out, your reputation will suffer. You have got to finish it within the next few days. Refuse, and I will make life difficult. I know you, aggro doesn't suit; it doesn't help the image to have your weaknesses aired publicly and particularly not on social media,' he threatens.

'You're bluffing, you think too much of Isabel to do that.'

Nicco moves closer to Max until they are facing each other eye to eye.

'Ask her what happened when she played the same game with that lawyer she was seeing. Ask her to tell you how long he spent in hospital, what one of her male cronies did to him and how long it took him to recover. Think carefully about what you do next, Max; make the wrong decision and you'll regret it. I'm not here for the fun of it. I'm your friend but you need to face the truth, even if that means getting heavy. Isabel is after the dirt on you, she knows there is something. She finds out, and your life will be in tatters. You do know that she met up with your PA, Alice, a couple of times. What do you imagine the pair talked about? Not about the weather, that's for sure.'

I doubt my aunt Nancy had anything in common with Isabel, so for her to spend time with her it must have been important. Something else to add to the growing list of things I need to know.

Nicco's plea to Max to wise up has had no effect. Max grabs hold of Nicco around his neck. Nicco lashes out and Max goes flying backwards. I hear Max's head hit the wooden floor in the hall and wince; that must have hurt. Their voices go up an octave as the argument enters a new phase. Nicco hauls Max to his feet and slams him against the wall. Max raises a fist and is ready to thump Nicco one when suddenly the grappling stops dead.

'I'm not joking, Max, I'll go to the police... I'll tell them what you did.'

Max looks terrified as Nicco pushes him away. 'We talked about this, you said to forget it, told me that it would never come out. What's changed, Nicco, why go back on your promise now?'

'That's down to you, Max. You fool around with my wife and expect me to do nothing?'

'I thought the pair of you were over, that's what Isabel told me.'

'It is over, but as much as Isabel needs her claws clipping, I don't want her hurt, and that's exactly what will happen if she keeps on seeing you. You need to wake up, it's your money she's after, Max. Think yourself lucky that she doesn't know your little secret because, old friend, if she did, you would have been bled dry by now.'

I want to know the *little secret*, whatever it is, myself. Did Alice know? Is that why the two talked? The mystery of Alice has no end to it.

Max stands up straight, runs a hand through his hair and shakes his head. 'No, Nicco, I'll give up Isabel in my own time. Say anything about what you know, and it'll be the last thing you do.'

That was a definite threat. I wish I knew what it was that Nicco knew about Max but I don't think it has anything to do with money. Would Max carry out his threat? I doubt it, too dangerous, and is he even capable of taking Nicco on?

I would soon find out to my cost that he's more than capable.

TWENTY-ONE

Nicco has gone and Max has disappeared. What just went on in the hallway was far too much for me; all I want now is the quiet of my own space.

'Are you okay, Donna?'

Tara. The last thing I want to do is make small talk with her, but I can at least give her the damn printouts I'm still clutching.

'Sorry you had to hear that. Men can be such hotheads at times.' She runs a hand through that lovely blonde hair of hers and smiles at me. I must be back in favour.

'I think we should have a chat,' she says.

Tara hasn't spoken to me since the restaurant debacle so I suppose we're due a chat. I can guess the first topic will be the incident at the door. I have no doubt she'll spout me some fairy story to gloss over what it was all about.

'I'm sure you heard Max and Nicco just now,' she begins. 'I don't want you to worry, it sounded worse than it is. They've been friends for a long time, and they always have these silly fallouts. Despite the threats, they wouldn't really harm each other, so I'm sure it will all blow over.'

That means she was listening too and has to have heard the

name *Isabel*. I want to ask her why Nicco was so wound up about Max seeing her but I hold back. It's a tricky one. Tara is the wronged woman and I don't think she'd appreciate me asking sensitive questions. It's none of my business anyway; as far as the family are concerned, I see nothing and say nothing.

'You remember Nicco, you met him at the wake,' she says. 'We know him well; he's an accountant and does works for Max occasionally. His beef today was about Max's business and profits; it'll be a tax thing, he's always on at Max about his expense claims. You do the day-to-day accounts but it's Nicco who has overall responsibility and files the tax return. It's only because he's an old friend that Max still puts up with his fussing.'

The argument didn't sound like an accounting problem to me, but if that's the way Tara wants it.

'I listened from behind the kitchen door,' she tells me. 'It all sounded much worse than it really is, and things never get nasty between Max and Nicco. Nicco's quick to lose it but soon cools down. I've known him a long time and, believe me, violence is not his thing.'

It didn't look like that to me, I thought he was going to do Max real damage at one point. I'm still clutching the printouts as I follow her into the sitting room. Taking them out of my hand, she gestures for me to sit down.

'Fancy a gin and tonic? After listening to that confrontation at the front door, I'm going to have one.'

This is the first time Tara has ever suggested we hang out, or shown any interest in me. I don't usually drink, but I can't miss this chance to ask her some questions, and to find out why she really wants to talk to me. She's in a good mood, so I jump at the chance.

'Thanks,' I reply.

'Are you happy here, Donna?'

That came out of the blue. What do I tell her? I can't admit that almost every day I consider leaving. Then there was the way she'd flown at me about both the dress and the necklace. Not the best way to keep an employee happy.

'I'm settling in.' It's pointless telling Tara anything different. That would only invite questions I don't have the energy to answer.

'I know I'm not easy to get on with.' She surprises me. 'There are reasons for that, which I can't explain to you, but rest assured, Donna, any criticism I make of you isn't meant as it sounds. The dress and the necklace, for example, I know you didn't take them. I know Max orchestrated the whole thing. Life with him isn't easy and not with Hanna either. She can be unpleasant, difficult to reach. If I'm honest, now she's grown up, she's more of a handful than she was as a toddler. I hope she's alright with you, that both her and Max don't cause you too much trouble.'

I don't understand why she's telling me all this; a deep and personal with Tara about her husband or daughter right now isn't what I want. But I have to say something.

'I get on with Hanna just fine.' A good start. 'As for Max, I suppose running a business is stressful, and people like Nicco don't help with their talk of going to the police.'

The words are out of my mouth before I can bite them back. Tara looks at me, that lovely face of hers pulled into a frown. *That was stupid*, I mentally scold myself. Now she'll go all moody on me; so much for that *chat*.

'The truth is both Nicco and I worry about Max's honesty. I know that he doesn't tell Nicco or you about every house sale. As you gain more experience of the business, you will realise. Suppliers' invoices with no matching sales to go with them. It used to worry Alice too, and she confronted him on it. But nothing changed; where Max is concerned, the money he makes has nothing to do with anyone but him.'

Her candour surprises me but I don't think the argument with Nicco was about money at all. Isabel was mentioned, so was a *secret*, something Nicco knows, something that could harm Max if it came out. Nicco said that Isabel was after Max's money, but in my opinion that was secondary to what the fight was really about. I just can't tell if Tara knows or not.

'Remember what I've told you, Donna. Not everything is as it seems. For now my advice is to keep your observations to yourself. Things happen in this house that we're not expected to notice or talk about. The exception to this is Hanna. She can be scathing when she wants to be. She once told Max that he was stubborn and cruel. That did her no good at all. You will have seen her room. The consequence of speaking her mind. He is a dangerous man; when things are really bad, he can't control his temper.'

She must be talking about Hanna's old room, the one she keeps locked and wouldn't let me see. Get Hanna in the right mood and I'll ask her to show me. It could help me understand how this family ticks. As for Max being dangerous, the jury's out on that one.

'Things will come right,' she assures me. 'They usually do.'

Both Max and Tara paint a bleak picture of family life. On the plus side, Tara has spoken to me about Max and Hanna and their faults, something I would never have expected. She hands me a large gin and tonic and right now I need it. I swallow a glug; it stings my throat and I realise it's mostly gin and short on tonic.

'Sorry, Tara, if I spoke out of turn.'

'You didn't. Your observations are correct. There is a lot wrong with Max's attitude to the business. Whatever you find out, keep it to yourself, don't say a word to Max or Hanna about this conversation either.'

Rising from the armchair, I walk across to the drinks cabinet and add more tonic to my drink. Gin isn't my favourite, particularly the way Tara serves it.

'I'm reluctant to tell tales, especially this one, but if I don't warn you, I'll regret it if anything happens to you.'

Happens to me... are things that bad?

'I know you tackled Max in the restaurant and that was brave of you, but he won't forget it. Don't give him the opportunity to retaliate. Max is good at taking his revenge slowly. I don't want you to fall foul of his temper again, so no prying questions, no comments about the business and you should be fine.'

'Is that what Alice did? Is that why she died?'

Tara looks me directly in the eyes. 'What happened to Alice was tragic,' she all but whispers. 'The coroner said accidental death due to anaphylactic shock, so we have no choice but to accept it.'

This explanation is very different from what I've been told and it puts an entirely different slant on the accident. The idea that it might have been someone's fault, Max's like Hanna suggested, has just gone out of the window.

'I thought she simply tripped and fell down the stairs. I had no idea there was a reason behind the fall.'

'Alice was allergic to peanuts. She ate a slice of cake that evening, not knowing what was in it. She screamed for help but it was too late. She always kept her EpiPen with her but not that night. She was on the stairs when she choked and fell.'

Tara takes a swallow of her gin, looks at me.

'She was all mixed up. I'm not surprised she lost the thing, and she was stressed out. Before she died, she told me that someone, a woman, had been pestering her. I think she was scared. I know Max told Alice to get rid of her.'

'Was it someone she knew?'

'I'm not sure; she was rough-looking, hard-faced, and not at all like someone I'd expect Alice to know.'

'You met her then?'

'Only briefly. She came to the door asking for Alice one day. I answered and told her that Alice wasn't in, and the woman got pretty nasty, threatening me and swearing. Then off she went and I never saw her again. It was all very strange.'

'Did Alice tell you anything about her?'

'She said the woman was collecting for a homeless shelter but I didn't believe a word of it. There was something about her that made me think she may have known Alice somehow. She was no youngster, in her mid-fifties, I would say, and she had the name *Alma* tattooed on the knuckles of her right hand.'

Hearing the name Alma had the power to freeze my very soul, and I struggled to remain straight-faced as the fear of that name rose in my chest. I didn't want Tara knowing the name Alma meant anything to me, so I didn't react, but memories of Alma are already screaming into my mind. She is the woman who threw me onto the street to fend for myself in the first place.

She is my mother.

TWENTY-TWO

Tara's description of the woman who'd pestered Alice was her sister Alma, my mother. The thought of her coming to this house fills me with dread. I hope and pray she doesn't come back.

Today has been tough and I have so much information whirling around my mind. Back in my rooms, I decide to have another go at cracking the memory stick password. I need to know what's going on here, and I doubt I'll be able to sleep anyway. I've jotted down a number of possibles. Given Alice, or Nancy, had lived in this house, I started with the names of the family. First Alice, then Max and Tara, even Hanna, but after ten minutes of trying them out, I have to face the fact that this isn't working. Alice could have used anything, and I don't have a clue.

I sit and stare at the stick and the paper it had been wrapped in. Donna Slade, I read, but it doesn't help. Curse Alice or Nancy, or whoever she was; if the stick is supposed to help me, why make it so damn difficult?

I try more words, even random ones – by now I'm desperate

– but have no luck. It should be simple, Nancy AKA Alice wanted me to have it. I must be missing something. I hold the stick in my hand again. Hoping for inspiration? This is stab-in-the-dark time.

I scrunch up the wrapping paper with my name on and aim for the bin. Then something strikes me, something that I'd dismissed when I first found the thing. Unravelling the paper, I see it clearly; the answer is suddenly obvious. There's no space between the *Donna* and *Slade*. My name is written as one string of letters. The elusive password isn't such a pain to find after all.

Back it goes into the USB slot, and lo and behold, it works. *DonnaSlade*, I can't believe I didn't spot it before.

I stare at the desktop. There is one folder and two documents on the stick. Clicking on one of them, I discover that it's password-protected too, and I soon find out so is the other one. Trying *DonnaSlade* doesn't work this time. Alice certainly hasn't made this bit easy either.

Only one folder is accessible. It's labelled *photos*.

I'll work on the other passwords later; for now I'll see what delights the folder holds. I just pray that it isn't a glimpse into my horrendous past.

As I double-click on the folder, the screen fills with images. Some of people, some of places, but all gut-wrenchingly familiar. My heart races and tears begin to well up.

The photo I look at first is of a group of people standing at the front of a terraced house. I study each face in turn and soon wish I hadn't. Staring back at me with blank, loveless eyes are photos of the few family members I had back then. My mother and two aunts... the only person missing is me. Taking a rough guess at the age of my mother, I would have been about sixteen – the age at which I was thrown out of the family home, living elsewhere and fending for myself. There was no sign of my father but that was to be expected; by the time I was born he was long gone.

Some images show the house where I lived as a child, others the streets I played in. On one was the shelter where I sought help when I was homeless. An interesting collection, some of which pose questions. The shelter, for example... at that time no one in my family knew where I was.

'What're you up to?' a familiar voice asks.

A shiver slips down my spine. Hanna has crept into my room, made me jump, and is now standing behind me, ogling the screen.

'Interesting stuff, people you know?'

Here she is again, peering over my shoulder, asking questions I don't want to answer.

'I'm busy, Hanna. Come back later?'

'If you want that box I bought for you then you'd better try harder. Being nice to me is a good place to start,' she taunts. 'Computer stuff, boring, you should ditch it and try having fun. You're a pain when you're all intense and serious.'

Insult delivered, she leaves my room, slamming the door behind her. *A pain*, that's rich coming from her. But she does have the wooden box, which, now that Nancy's dead, rightly should be mine. But her mood has changed since earlier; helpful Hanna is now difficult Hanna who doesn't want to help at all.

'Tone down the noise, Hanna,' I shout after her.

'You've pissed me off now,' she shrieks back.

I don't have time to deal with her, I have work to do.

'Okay, point taken,' says a voice from behind me.

She's back and staring over my shoulder again. It's unnerving how she can enter a room so quietly.

'I'm sorry. I'll give you the box, don't worry.' She points to the image I'm staring at. 'Who are they?'

I force a smile. 'My family.' *Family*: I don't want to call them that but I don't want to be interrogated by Hanna either. 'That's my mother.' Hanna says nothing. I point to someone else. 'And that's Alice, or Nancy. D'you recognise her?'

She recognised her alright. I could tell by the look of surprise on her face.

'She's a lot younger but that's definitely Alice. If this is your family, does that mean Alice is a relative of yours?'

'My mother's sister, my aunt, and her name is Nancy not Alice. From now on that's what I want to call her.'

'Why would your aunt come to live and work here under a false name?'

Good question but I don't have an answer. If I did it would go a long way to solving the damn mystery I'm mixed up in.

Alice is Nancy, there is no doubt about that, but what happened to make her computer savvy and pass herself off as a competent PA? The Nancy I knew had little education to speak of and worked in a shoe factory.

'I've no idea why she chose to work for your father, but she must have had a reason.'

'I didn't think our Alice could be so devious.'

Devious, yes, I put that down to a family trait. But to fool the Marsden family like she did amazes me.

'She was your aunt; you must have had some idea what she was up to?'

'I didn't, and why would I? I haven't seen her or any of my family in years. The woman who worked here, the woman you and your parents described to me, isn't the woman I remember.'

'You could be lying,' Hanna said, and I immediately resented her for it. 'You find out Nancy's dead and come here to collect the money in her bank account. You see where I'm going. The tale you spun about the email, not knowing she'd taken your name, is a lie. That would work, don't you think?'

What a load of rubbish, but I'm too tired to rise to the bait.

'Why would I think Nancy had any money? She had nothing when I knew her.'

'She had money alright, about two hundred thousand.'

'She had this job and that's it. She couldn't have more than a few quid squirrelled away, not the small fortune you're talking about.'

'You're wrong,' she tells me with worrying certainty.

'Okay, Hanna, suppose she did; where did it come from?'

'She was blackmailing Max.'

TWENTY-THREE

'That's some accusation, Hanna. Do you have any proof to back it up?'

The Nancy I knew was as honest as the day is long; that can't be said about others in my family. Whatever the reason my aunt came here and used my name, it had nothing to do with money. Of that I'm sure.

'It's only a theory; I could be totally wrong, but if I am, I'm sorry,' Hanna says.

'Then why say it at all?'

'I know precious little about you. You could be up to anything, in cahoots with this Nancy until she died for all I know.'

I could let rip, speak my mind, but with this young woman it'd achieve nothing. Better to keep quiet and let her ramble on.

'Nancy was secretive. I've no idea what went on in that head of hers, but pretending to be someone else is weird.'

My thoughts exactly; mind you, I've no right to talk.

'Remember, don't tell your parents yet. I've got other stuff to think about and don't have the time to explain that one.'

'That's another favour, Donna. They're adding up.'

'Look, Hanna, none of this is my fault. Nancy came here and used a different name, I have no idea why.'

'She must have had a reason, and I don't believe that you don't know what that is.'

Hanna is totally wrong. I can't read her and can't decide which of the versions she believes: that I was enticed here by an anonymous email or that it was part of some plan to take what Nancy had stolen from Max.

'Nancy never said anything about having a family, and that includes you. I did ask her if she had relatives but she always dodged the question.'

Nancy didn't want to talk of her family either. At least we had that in common.

'Max gave her a job, and within a few weeks he was doing as she told him. That's way out of character for him. So you see, the only explanation I can think of is that he was scared of her. Now you know my theory, do you have a better one?'

Scared. I doubt Max knows the meaning of the word.

'Right now, I don't. Does it matter now anyway? Nancy's dead and no threat to anyone, your father included.'

'Nancy did have money,' Hanna says. 'Like I said, from Max.'

'How can you be sure that she had money, did she tell you?'

'She used online banking. Then, one day when she was logged into it, she was called away and forgot to log out. I was quick, but I had enough time to take a good look, and she had a sizeable amount put away in a savings account.'

That surprises me. She did my job, and more than likely was paid the same, so where did the money come from? Could Hanna be right? Was she in fact blackmailing Max?

'Nancy found out something about Max, something big, and tried to bleed him dry.'

'Is anyone else involved in whatever it is Max is up to?'

'Isabel, she is bound to be. That's why she clings to Max like a limpet. I hate that woman,' Hanna tells me. 'I mean, really hate her; the woman is a first-class bitch. Whenever I see her outside, or Max sneaks her into the house when Tara's out, she completely ignores me. Never once has Max introduced us; he's afraid I'll say something to Tara.'

'Did Nancy know about the affair?'

'She would have known all along about Isabel. Nancy was sneaky, she read his text messages whenever she got the chance. Max has a habit of leaving his phone on the hall table when he's in the house, making it easy enough to do.'

'If this was blackmail, do you think Tara would know there's money missing from their accounts?'

'Head in the sand, that's Tara. Even if she has a suspicion that Max is up to something, she'd rather forget about it than take him on. Tara wouldn't notice missing money anyway. Max is in property sales. High-class stuff. His company, Marsden Holdings, builds houses in the expensive areas of Cheshire and the Lakes. The money comes rolling in, far more than they can spend.'

'Do you know Nicco?'

'Yeah, although I only know of him; we've never actually spoken. He comes to the house sometimes, but he's someone else they've never introduced me to. It's Tara who told me his name. She told me he's a scary man and she doesn't trust him.'

Not what she told me.

All talk of where Nancy got her money from ends as Hanna points to the photo of my family on the laptop.

'In the photo, your mother is holding a baby. Whose is it?'

She's right. I lean forward; the image is blurred, which is how I must have missed it. The only regret I ever had about leaving my family is that the infant had to stay behind. God knows what upbringing she had. My eyes fill with tears. I don't want Hanna to see me weeping but I can't help it. I reach out and trace round the image with a finger. The baby is wrapped in a pink blanket with a teddy bear motif on one corner. A long time ago, I bought one exactly like it.

TWENTY-FOUR

Memories of my youth always make me sad. I wish things had been different, that my family had been pleasant, kind people who'd cared for each other. But given my mother's temperament, that was never going to happen. The baby in her arms in the photo is testament to that. When I heard that it had been born, I bought the blanket as a gift. I have no idea why my mother has hold of the infant; it certainly wasn't hers.

I wade through the images. A number of them are me in various stages of growing up. Others show the house I lived in as a child. Others the streets I played in. But the one of the homeless shelter I used during the colder months startled me. How had Nancy found that one? If she knew where I was, why not approach me? I'd have loved to have seen her and been able to keep in touch.

Reminiscing isn't good for me; I'm sat here with tears in my eyes. The past is gone, out of reach, and no amount of wishful thinking will bring it back. I was treated badly, my mother never wanted me and made me pay, it was as simple as that.

I'm not going to finish the search tonight. I'm not in the

mood. Better to get a night's sleep and start again tomorrow, and this time I'll leave the photo folder well alone.

I close the laptop lid. 'I'm sorry, Hanna, but I can't look at any more.'

'I'll see you tomorrow then.'

'Don't forget I still need that wooden box.'

'Stop stressing, you'll get it, don't worry.'

I give her a nod of thanks and see her through the door. I need to be on my own. I'm not good company anyway; there's too much going on in my head. Hopefully a good night's sleep will help to wash some of it away.

I had no chance of getting a good night's sleep, and I toss and turn until the early hours. I know much more now about the woman this family knew as Alice but I've no idea why I'm here or what I'm supposed to find. Hanna thinks money. I hope she's right and that Nancy lured me here to find it, but it would have been simpler to leave it to me in her will.

That begs another question: if Nancy did blackmail Max, was that a motive for killing her? Was he even capable of doing that? Hanna thinks so. I've seen him angry, fight back when challenged, but murder is something else. And what did she know that was so big she could get away with blackmailing him?

I must have fallen asleep, and the next thing I know, I'm being awakened by banging on my door. Grabbing a dressing gown, I go to see what's so urgent.

It's Hanna. Pale-faced, wide-eyed and obviously in a state about something.

'I've just seen Isabel walking up the drive.'

I check the time, it's only five in the morning, for goodness' sake.

'Are you sure it's her?'

'It's her, I do know what she looks like. I've seen her before at the various functions Max and Tara have dragged me to.'

'But you've never actually met her?'

'I told you, Max wouldn't dare introduce her to me. Too scared of what I might say. Max will be livid that she's come here, but not with Isabel, oh no, she can do no wrong. It makes no sense, but he'll twist things, blame everyone else, me in particular.'

'Do you have any idea what she could possibly want?'

'To confront Max perhaps, make him tell Tara the relationship is serious... truth is it could be anything.'

Hanna is rattled and isn't sure what to do. Neither am I. The pair of us staying well out of it is the best idea.

'We should let them fight it out amongst themselves. It could be dangerous for us to get involved.'

Hanna looks at me and shakes her head.

'Don't you want to know what's going on? I'll never forgive myself if I miss any of the action. We could risk it, go down and have some fun.'

She's got a strange idea of what constitutes fun! The last thing I want to do is witness all-out war between those three. But before I can stop her, Hanna is already on the staircase. I can't let her do this alone. Pulling my dressing gown tight around my frame, I follow.

Isabel, Max and Tara are stood in the hall; the argument is in full flow. Neither me nor Hanna should be here. This is none of our business. I, for one, don't want to be dragged into a family row.

It's obvious Isabel has said something to Tara. The anger on her face tells me that. Max is pacing, unsure what to say or do. I feel for Tara. Tonight she's had to face Max's infidelity full-on and come to terms with the fact that it's real and not just coincidence or in her mind.

'Morning everyone,' Hanna says brazenly.

Her tone sounds normal, even casual, as if it's no big deal to find the three of them like this. I watch as she looks from one to the other, a grin on her face.

'Things look serious, should I be worried?' she jokes. 'Say the word and we can start again. This time you can all smile at me as I come down the stairs. But it might be an idea to stop the bawling and screaming first.'

I wince at her tone. She's certainly got some nerve, I'll give her that. I can't describe the look on Tara's face, but if I had to, I'd say murderous.

'You shouldn't be here,' Max barks at her. 'Go back to your room.'

Hanna ignores him and looks straight at Isabel. 'I don't believe we've been introduced.'

Hanna has jumped right in; this is beyond embarrassing.

'It's not what it seems,' Max tells her.

Tara is watching this with wild eyes blazing anger.

'It never is, Max. Do you want to tell us all what is going on? The truth, mind you, not some half-baked excuse.'

Max's eyes narrow. He says nothing but I bet he's raging inside. He grabs Isabel's hand and tugs her towards the front door.

'Isabel is an accountant and a friend, she's here on business, nothing else. Get back to your room, Hanna, and stay there.'

'I'm twenty-three, not three. You've no right to tell me what to do.'

'Hanna, none of this is your business and believe me, you're better off out of it.'

Tara pipes up. 'Get that woman out of here, Max, or I will.'

This has nothing to do with me. I wish now that I'd let Hanna go it alone and stayed upstairs.

'Look what you've done, Hanna. You storm into the middle of a disagreement, upsetting everyone. Look at Tara, she's traumatised.'

'This is down to you, Max. You're the one in the wrong here,' Hanna taunts him. 'Who is she anyway? And don't spout that business nonsense at me.'

Hanna's really going for it now. She should stop before she goes too far but she's on a roll.

'This is stupid; you know very well who Isabel is.'

'Why should I? A friend, you said, so why hasn't she been here before and why haven't you introduced us?'

'You've really done it this time, Max. We can't get over this. You will pack some things and get out of my sight. I'm sick and tired of looking at you and pretending this sordid affair isn't going on. I don't want to see you in this house again,' yells an angry Tara.

Ignoring his wife, Max faces Hanna.

'I'm sorry that you've had to witness this.'

'I bet you are,' she says.

'Okay, you want an introduction, do you?' Max spits the words at Hanna. 'This is Isabel. Happy now?'

He turns to Tara and shakes his head. 'I've asked Isabel to take over from Nicco as company accountant, that's all, Tara. You are letting your imagination run away with you if you think anything else.'

'That's a lie and you know it. You've been seeing that bitch for months.'

Hanna gives Tara a nod. 'She's right. Why not come clean, Max, and stop denying it?'

I watch Hanna move closer to Isabel, look her up and down and then straight in the eye.

'No one else is going to do the introductions so I'll make them myself. I'm Hanna.' She smiles at Isabel. 'And you must be the bitch who's fucking my dad.'

TWENTY-FIVE

All hell lets loose. Tara dissolves into tears. Isabel gasps, gives Hanna a vicious clout across the face before retreating to the front door. Hanna stands still, hands on her hips with a deepening red patch on her cheek.

'Once you've sorted this mess, ring me,' Isabel shouts at Max. 'Once I'm happy your family won't lynch me, we'll talk terms.'

Max puts an arm around Tara. 'You need to calm down or you'll make yourself ill.'

'Get off me. I don't want to calm down. Leave me alone, Max... the mood I'm in, I'll bloody kill you.'

Tara's vicious, and from the look on her face, she means it.

'Why don't you go after her? Go on, you have my blessing because I certainly don't want you.'

'This is stupid,' Max tells her. 'Isabel is a colleague, nothing more. You've got this all wrong.'

'Get out of my sight. I can't stand to look at you.'

An exasperated Max takes hold of Hanna's arm and leads her towards the front door.

'We need a chat,' he tells her. 'We'll have a walk round the garden in the fresh air and sort this.'

I only came downstairs because of the shouting; I was concerned that someone was hurt. Now I wish I'd stayed put, although I did enjoy the way Hanna tackled Isabel. Mind you, the fallout from this won't be pleasant.

How the family come back from this is anybody's guess. If I was Tara, I know what I'd do. I'd kick Max out, lick my wounds and not look back. But she won't, and, anyway, Max will have none of it; he's already made excuses about his relationship with Isabel. Tara will have her doubts, label Isabel a home-wrecker, and life will continue as normal.

With Isabel gone, Hanna and Max wandering around outside, me and Tara share an uncomfortable silence. I'm about to retreat to my rooms when she decides to speak.

'This is what Hanna and I have to put up with, Donna. Max has asked that woman here tonight to upset me and has the cheek to call her a colleague. Who is he kidding? That woman is a lot of things, but *colleague*? Never in a million years.'

I don't comment. I mean, what can I say? It looks like Tara is right. She must be; it's unlikely that both she and Hanna are wrong.

'It's only a matter of time before he pushes me out. He'll bring her here, make some excuse why she has to stay, and she'll never leave.'

Tears are running down Tara's face as she talks. She's hiding nothing, her eyes are red and her cheeks blotchy. She's on the edge, terrified of losing Max, hating Isabel and powerless to do anything about it.

'You saw what happened, the pair of them swapping those knowing looks. Hanna shouldn't have said what she did; it was vulgar, but she was right.'

Brave of her, is what I thought. Given that Max is the villain in all this, I am worried about her. They went outside a good fifteen minutes ago and haven't come back in yet.

'Max wouldn't hurt Hanna?' I ask, hoping she'd think the question ridiculous, but she doesn't.

There's more weeping and head shaking before she wails, 'I don't know. Max is quick to defend Isabel, making everything someone else's fault and never hers. He gets angry when we criticise their relationship and call the woman names. Hanna made a big mistake tonight and he won't forgive her for it.'

'I'm going to take a look, make sure Hanna is okay.'

'Don't,' Tara warns. 'It won't go well for any of us if Max thinks you're interfering. Leave them, it's safer.'

Safer for who? Certainly not Hanna. Disregarding Tara's advice, I hurry to the front door and out onto the drive. I take a quick look around but there is no sign of either of them in the front garden.

It takes five minutes to circle the house. I look in the shed and take a walk past the pig pen, but nothing. Both Max's car and Tara's are still in the garage. They've both vanished into thin air.

'Do you know of anywhere they can be?' I ask Tara once back inside. 'They're nowhere to be seen.'

'Don't worry,' she assures me. 'They'll have gone for a walk to talk things over. Max will be telling Hanna not to behave like that again and how I've got it all wrong. She might take some convincing but eventually she'll agree with him.'

I have my doubts. That was some bust-up, and it'll take some putting right. Tara is dabbing at her eyes; the tears have stopped and her attention is elsewhere. She keeps checking her watch, and her eyes flick back and forth from me to her mobile on the coffee table.

'Are you expecting a call?'

'Someone who's looking for a property on a new development said they'd ring this evening and talk it over with Max.'

'Wouldn't they normally go through an estate agency?'

'Yes, but this is someone Max knows, so he's making an exception.'

I feel I should sit with Tara, keep her company until Max and Hanna return, but I'm too tired. A couple of hours and it'll be time to open the office.

'I'm off to bed,' I tell her. 'See you later perhaps.'

She says nothing, gives me a half-hearted smile, and reaches for the gin. Poor Tara, I feel for her; life isn't easy with Max for a husband.

TWENTY-SIX

I retreat to my rooms. No one is really interested in me or my opinion anyway. This is a family thing and ideally I want no part in it. Both Tara and Hanna have every right to be angry. Max should know better than to flaunt his mistress in front of his family. But Hanna's reaction, the show she put on, isn't clever. Havoc is all very well but there will be consequences, that I'm sure of. I'm concerned about her. Hanna's good at upsetting people; if what Tara has told me about Max being dangerous is true then Hanna could be in trouble. I'm not saying she's wrong – both Max and Tara have told me that Hanna has problems – but tonight she's gone to the brink, and there's no telling how Max will retaliate.

* * *

I woke up late; last night I'd sat up in bed for ages with the laptop on my knee trying to solve the problem of the passwords, but I must have nodded off, and now it's 9 a.m. the next morning.

A shower and change of clothes later, and I'm ready to face

a day in the office with Max and Tara, provided they've not killed each other. I soon discover that work isn't an option; both offices are locked and I don't have the key. And that's not the only thing: there is no noise coming from downstairs. No morning bustle, no radio and no voices. In fact, the house is eerily quiet. I creep down the stairs with the intention of seeing if there is anyone in the sitting room or perhaps the garden, but Maria stops me at the kitchen door.

'Do you want breakfast?'

Things are too weird to think of food. I shake my head. The truth is I couldn't eat a thing, not until I find out if Hanna is okay.

'Have you seen Hanna this morning?'

'I haven't seen her since yesterday.'

Short and sweet. 'What about Max and Tara, have you seen them?'

'No, it is only you for breakfast. The others are not here, they must have gone out early.'

I have a horrible feeling about this. Where could they be? Are they even safe?

'Did they leave a message for me about work today, a note, anything?'

'I have not been told anything but Mrs Marsden will be back shortly.'

'Do you know where she's gone?'

'She was up and about early, said she was going out for a walk to clear her head. I haven't seen Mr Marsden.'

I can understand that. Tara has had a tough time and, with what Maria has just said, she can't have got any sleep after I left her.

'I'll just have a cup of coffee, please, Maria.' I smile at her. I follow her into the kitchen. I've never actually had a conversation with the woman. She's always seemed standoffish, even amused by me. 'I can't believe I've been here for a week and we haven't really had a chance to talk. Have you been here long?'

'Three months,' she replies, which surprises me. The way she runs this kitchen, I thought she'd been here years.

'Are you enjoying the job?'

'Not really, these people are odd. They're not like other families I've worked for.'

Fair enough, my thoughts too. 'Will you stay here?'

'No, I don't think so. I have a sister in York; she has a bakery and a small shop. She's asked me to work with her. I've told Mrs Marsden that I'll work until the end of the month.'

She hands me the coffee and gives me another smile; we're almost getting on. I walk off towards the sitting room. It's empty but the French doors are open, swinging in the breeze. Sipping my coffee, I go to close them when I see Tara sitting out on the patio.

'Morning,' I call to her. 'I came looking for you, to ask for the office key, but Maria said you were out.'

'Never mind the office today. I'm sure you're not in the mood for work any more than I am.'

She's right there. I sit down opposite her; from the state of her I'd say she'd spent the time since I saw her last weeping. Her cheeks are streaked with mascara and her hair is a mess, this is not the usual Tara at all.

'Have you heard from Hanna?'

'I haven't seen her since last night. After her outburst, she was upset and didn't want to come home. She messaged to say she's gone to stay with a friend of hers for a few days. She'll ring when she wants to come back.'

That's weird. Hanna told me she didn't have any friends and that's why she clung to Nancy, so who is she staying with and why did she lie to me?

'What about Max...? Have you heard from him?'

She starts weeping again and shakes her head.

'He'll have gone to *her*,' she says, her disdain evident. 'I hate him for it. Why I ever loved him in the first place is a mystery. I knew he wasn't right from the start of our relationship. He's picky, controlling and has a short fuse. You wouldn't believe what he's put Hanna and me through over the years. Even when Hanna was a child, he tormented her ruthlessly. He never wanted children, see. He told me right from the start that he wasn't parent material. I took no notice. I loved him back then and was sure he didn't mean it. I thought that within a year or two of our marriage he'd change his mind.'

I see now that's the reason behind Max's pitiless behaviour towards the pair of them.

'At times he's fine, the perfect husband and father, but it doesn't last.'

'But he wouldn't *hurt* her?' I emphasise the word hurt, and Tara responds with yet more tears.

She shakes her head. 'He's more subtle than that. There's a locked room upstairs.'

'The one next to Hanna's bedroom.'

'Has Hanna shown you inside?'

'No, she told me it's always kept locked.'

'Come with me and I'll show you. It will help to make you understand, to prove that I'm not simply making all this up.'

That had occurred to me, but to be honest, I'm lost. 'Nose-in-the-air' Tara I can cope with, but not this version. She's all over the place, emotional, weeping and confessing all that is wrong with her marriage.

'At first I didn't believe my own eyes. I would never have believed that Max could be so cruel. But I was wrong. The man is a monster.'

TWENTY-SEVEN

Just before we enter, she turns to look at me.

'This was Hanna's domain for most of her childhood, up until she was seventeen. It was then she rebelled and threatened to leave. It was only then that Max relented and allowed her to have the room next door. This room has been left as it is, a warning to Hanna not to push things too far.'

The pain in her voice throws me. This is uncomfortable; as curious as I am, I'd give anything to be somewhere else.

Tara doesn't use a key to unlock the room but slips a heavy bolt across. It strikes me that it would be a simple matter to lock someone in. That thought makes me shiver.

'You should know that everything you see has nothing to do with me or Hanna,' she sobs. 'What's behind this door is all Max's work.'

Curiosity piqued, I follow her. I don't know what I expected but not this.

If I had to liken the room to anything, it would be a prison cell. There is one window which is boarded up with wooden slats and lets in little natural light. There is no carpet on the floor, not even a mat by the bed, just the original wooden boards. Hanging from the ceiling is a single bulb with no shade. The walls are painted a dull grey and there is little furniture. I have seen some dismal, soul-destroying accommodation in my time but this space is one of the worst.

'You're shocked,' Tara says, taking my hand. 'Sometimes Hanna was kept in here for days on end. All Max allowed her to eat was dry bread and water.'

'She was a prisoner in her own home?'

'That's exactly what she was. Hanna was alone, with none of the comforts she was used to, and little food.'

I walk around the room, taking in the contents. A bed, no sheets or duvet, just a bare mattress that's seen better days. An old dressing table stands against one wall, scuffed and with the mirror hanging off its hinges. It's a dreadful place, dirty, uncomfortable and not fit for anyone to sleep in.

'There is a small shower and toilet in the alcove over there.'

I take a look and wish I hadn't; the place hasn't been cleaned in ages and all there is for privacy is an old, tattered curtain.

I turn to Tara; she's weeping again. 'Could Hanna not call for help, or ring one of her friends and tell them where she was?'

'She'd scream all night long but Max didn't blink an eye. As for contacting anyone, the first thing he'd do when he threw her in here was confiscate her mobile.'

I can't believe Max would lock his child in here; it's inhumane. Nothing she did, no matter how upsetting, deserves this.

'What you see is bad enough, but this isn't the worst of it, Donna.' She bends down and pulls a length of thick chain from under the bed. 'See that metal loop hanging from the beam up there?' She rattles the chain then throws it to the floor. 'He used it to chain her up whenever she argued or tried to fight back. This is not a bedroom by any stretch of the imagination. The room is nothing but a prison cell, and over the years it's been well used.'

How can Max be so cruel? How could a parent, someone who is supposed to love and protect her, do this? I feel sick; no way does the girl deserve this. This is a world away from anywhere else in this house.

'Max tormented Hanna for years when she was younger. Any word out of place, any look she gave him that he didn't like, and this became her living hell for days. There was nothing I could do. He threatened to lock me in here if I breathed a word to anyone.'

I'm struggling with this. I can't believe what I'm hearing or the sight in front of my eyes. Tara stands by my side, tears falling down her cheeks. My heart goes out to her. I want to help, try to put this right, but I have no influence with Max, and Tara is too afraid. Hanna has a wonderful home but it is a shame about her parents. This room is testament to how vindictive Max can be.

I'm truly shocked and don't want to believe that Max would do this or that Tara would let him, but the proof is all around me. This is truly one mixed-up family.

'This room is only the tip of the iceberg,' Tara continues. 'After Hanna was forced into this room, he confiscated her clothes. He left her with two pairs of jeans, a few t-shirts and clothes that didn't fit her anymore.'

I want to help, but realistically, what can I do?

In the few days I've known Max, I've witnessed one small outburst in the car and the incident in the restaurant when he tried to browbeat me into admitting I was in the wrong about the dress.

The solitary world Hanna has lived in must have been hard on her. My parents were crap too, we have that in common. I lived in fear without the trappings of wealth.

My head is crammed with bad memories, the neglect, the indifference, but goodness knows what Hanna's head is full of.

My family had their failings, big ones, but at least they didn't deliberately set out to harm me.

Tara must know how much this has affected her daughter. Hanna is a complex young woman with issues, and who can blame her? This bedroom is a dark, cruel place; it's a dreadful way to punish anyone, never mind your own child. My first impression of her parents was obviously wrong. The way this family live is unnatural. I'm out of my depth, not only with how to deal with Hanna but with Max too.

'We should leave,' Tara says. 'Being in here does no one any good.'

I can't begin to think what state Hanna must have been in when Max slammed that door shut and pushed the bolt home. She must have fought with that door, pulling, pushing in her desperation to get out.

I'm confused, I don't know who I can trust anymore. Tara is weak; she won't stand up to Max. Max, he has to be some sort of psychopath. I certainly can't trust that he won't treat me any better than Hanna if I cross some imaginary line.

'When did Hanna get her new bedroom?'

'Two years ago. Max relented on her twenty-first birthday. Hanna threatened to leave if things weren't put right. Max knew that if she did, Hanna wouldn't hesitate in telling anyone who'd listen what her father did to her.'

I'm surprised that she put up with Max's tyranny for so long. As I've seen for myself, she is capable of voicing her opinions. Her fear of Max had certainly taken a holiday in the early hours of this morning.

'I could do with a gin,' Tara says. 'I know it's only morning but I don't care. I need something to help me sleep.'

We leave the room and Tara bolts the door. I'll accompany her back to the sitting room, get her that drink then return to my room.

'Would you mind getting me my pills?' Tara asks. 'They're in the dressing table drawer in our bedroom.'

I don't know what she takes; something for anxiety or depression is the impression I got, but I do wonder if she should be swallowing pills and downing gin at the same time.

I've not been in Max and Tara's bedroom before, and not surprisingly, it's every bit as spectacular as the rest of the house. But I'm not here to gawp; a quick rummage through the drawer and I find the pills. There is no label on the bottle, nothing to say where it was dispensed either. I have only ever swallowed the odd aspirin for a headache so I'm no expert. I remove the top and take a closer look. The tablets are small, white and with nothing written on them. I've no idea what they are supposed to be, but I know what they are.

The giveaway is the strong smell of peppermint. They are not pills at all; they're sweets.

TWENTY-EIGHT

Is Tara deliberately lying to her family about needing pills or has Max changed them and she doesn't know? If he has, then surely Tara would realise what she was swallowing; I certainly would. I can't think why Max would do that, but so many things happen in this house that I can't work out, so best leave it.

Pills delivered, and gin bottle and glass placed on the coffee table in front of her, I take refuge back in my rooms.

If there is a good side to all this, it gives me an opportunity to look at those two documents on the memory stick. Nancy set them up for a reason; I need to read them and find out why. The sooner I can work out what's going on here, the sooner I can leave and get away from this family forever. I could leave now, take the stick and disappear, but I'll still have questions, the truth about Nancy's death, for instance.

I fire up my laptop, insert the stick and sit back while it loads. This has to be the umpteenth time I've stared at the screen, wondering what to do next. If Nancy has left me something, be it money or not, surely she wouldn't make finding it so difficult. Like with the memory stick password, I must be missing something. The answer is probably staring me in face;

I just can't see it. The two documents have the names *One* and *Two*. I need a clue but have no idea where to look. In the folder with the photos in it, perhaps. I don't want to look at them again, but if Nancy has left a clue, perhaps that's where it is.

Images of my family, the house we lived in, even the hostel that took me in are all there, but what is their significance? If there is any, that is. Nancy knew how I felt about my family so why shove them down my throat like this? Perhaps she thought I'd mellowed a little. No chance. I hate that house and everyone in it. The neglect, the indifference, changed me, and I've carried the mental scars ever since.

Feeling sorry for myself won't get this mystery solved. There's a clue amongst these images, there has to be. What I need is inspiration, like with the memory stick's password. I cracked that one eventually, even though it was obvious once I found it.

The slam of the front door rattles the whole house and I jump in my seat. Max is back.

Closing the laptop, I fearfully creep to the door to listen as Tara screams at him in the hallway.

'Get a grip, Tara,' he tells her. 'You're half cut and it's not yet lunchtime.'

I hear him hurrying up the stairs and then his office door bang shut. I should speak to him, at least ask about Hanna, but I'm scared. Tara painted a bleak picture of him, and after what I've seen, I have to accept that he's one scary man. The decision to speak to him or not is taken out of my hands when he calls my name.

Taking a deep breath, I leave the relative safety of my rooms and go to see what he wants. Surprise, surprise, he actually ushers me into *his* office. That exclusive room I was warned never to enter on pain of death. Well, not quite, but that's how it sounded when Tara spelled things out to me. The anger he exhibited downstairs has disappeared to be replaced by nice Max, the one I used to like.

'I need a few things getting together,' he starts. 'I'm off to Spain in a few days. I'm checking on some properties we've had built in Marbella.' He smiles at me. 'I have to say I'm looking forward to the change of scene and the relative peace.'

He's going away, none of us here will miss him. A few days isn't long enough; I, for one, wish he wasn't coming back.

'I'll need my passport finding and some documents printing out.'

'The documents are no problem, but your passport, where do I start?'

He turns on the charm and gives me *one of those smiles* then hands me a key.

'It's for the safe. It should be in there, but if it isn't, have a search round the office. It could be in one of my desk drawers. Once you're finished, put the key in the small money box you'll find in the left-hand drawer of my desk.'

My eyes wander to the huge metal thing stood against one wall. It looks so old it could have come out of the ark. Still, I bet it's strong, and without a key, it would be a bugger to open. But I am flattered that he trusts me. That could come in handy at some point.

I wave the key at him. 'Is there a combination too?'

'It's second-hand, and whoever had it before us had the safe altered. All that's needed to open it now is that key.'

Dare I ask? I might as well while he's in such a good mood.

'Is Hanna okay?' Several seconds of silence later, he nods.

'She's fine, out of harm's way, and that's the important thing, especially to me away.'

No details then, no mention of exactly where she is. 'Has she got her mobile?'

'No, I took it off her. After what happened, I don't want either Tara or Isabel giving her a hard time.'

No mobile, so no contact. He is her father, and ordinarily I wouldn't worry, but this is a weird situation, particularly as she is an adult. It makes me wonder if Hanna is really out of *harm's way* or if that's a euphemism for him holding her prisoner somewhere. That popped into my head because of the way things are and what Tara has shown me. Hanna's room is a disgrace and he should be thoroughly ashamed of himself.

'Look, I've still got things to see to and need to go out. Can you have the documents ready for when I get back, say an hour?'

'I'll get on with them straight away,' I assure him.

'If my passport isn't in there'—he nods at the safe—'have a rummage through my desk drawers and see if you can find it.'

I can't believe this; he's literally given me permission to search his office.

'An hour then, I shouldn't be any longer.'

Another smile and he's gone. I hear him hurry down the corridor then the front door bang shut. No further arguments with Tara, then.

First, the safe. I have to say this is exciting, who knows what secrets it contains. Max's passport should be top of the list but I will find other stuff, paperwork certainly, and, if I'm lucky, something to help me unravel the mystery of Nancy. I've no idea what but I have to be optimistic.

I kneel in front of the safe, steady my hand and go for it. A turn of the key and I'm in. One sigh of relief later sees me rifling through the pile of paperwork Max has stashed in here, boring stuff, contracts and the like, but no sign of a passport. There is an ornate silver jewellery box. I run my fingers over it then take a peek. It contains some of Tara's jewellery, probably the more valuable pieces, not what I'm after. There is a second box at the back, large, black and made of tin. Dragging it closer, I lift the lid; it contains several certificates, one of them is Max and Tara's marriage certificate, but no passport.

But there is a mobile phone. It's an old one, nothing like the super-duper, all-singing, all-dancing model Max currently has in his pocket. Is this a burner phone? Why would Max have one? Leaving it in the safe, I can understand, but why give me the key? The only reason I can think of is that he has forgotten the phone is here. Surprisingly, it isn't password-protected, and I take a look at what's on it. There are several photos, mostly of Tara and Hanna, of places they've been. But it's the text messages that interest me. This could be the phone he uses to contact Isabel. I know I shouldn't but I'm already in a world of trouble. I'm right, there is lots of work stuff going on, but nothing lovey-dovey, which surprises me. There are messages from other people too, customers, I presume.

And then I see it. Tara was right about the woman who came to the door. I'm looking at a message from Alma, my mother, to Max. I'm shaking as I read it. How does Max know her, and what could they possibly have to text about?

'What do you think you're doing?' asks a male voice behind me. I've been caught snooping and have no excuse at the ready.

TWENTY-NINE

I'm paralysed, rooted to the spot, kneeling in front of the safe. I have Max's permission to search through the contents, but it's the voice that came from behind me that has me rooted in fear. With the phone in my hand, I turn and face him.

'Nicco,' I manage, when my voice finally works. 'What are you doing here?'

'I could ask you the same question.'

'Max asked me to look for his passport,' I say as casually as I can, as if rifling through the safe and stealing a mobile is no big deal. 'He gave me the key.' I wave it in front of him.

'He's going somewhere?'

'I believe so but I've no idea where,' I lie. Although I can't explain why, it's just a feeling that something isn't right and things would be better if I kept it to myself.

Nicco nods and points to Max's desk.

'He used to keep it in a folder in the top right-hand drawer; it's the folder marked *personal*.'

I get to my feet, give Nicco a smile, walk across to the desk and open the drawer. Right enough, there is a folder and, bingo, Max's passport is there. Nicco still hasn't said anything about the phone. He can't have seen me take it then and most likely thinks it's mine.

'Thanks, I could have searched all afternoon and not found it.'

'I doubt that, Donna. We both know that's not what would have happened; you're a resourceful young woman.'

There is something about the look on his face and the way he said that. It's as if he knows damn well what I'm up to, and not just with the mobile either. I want rid of him before he starts asking questions.

'Are you looking for Max?'

'Yes, but it'll wait. Would you ask him to give me a ring when you next see him?'

We smile at each other, and he's gone. I finally take a deep breath. Nicco is difficult to read. He stands there, a giant of a man peering down at everyone around him and giving you the feeling that he knows what's going on inside your head, and that includes me. Despite my doubts, I want to get on with him. Getting on the wrong side of Nicco is not wise, as I gathered from our talk at the wake. He knows some dangerous people but that's another conversation we will no doubt have one day. But for now, I've other things to think about.

I can't wait to get back to the privacy of my rooms and look at those messages on the mobile. To be honest, they're all I can think about. Max and Alma, now there's a strange mix. The connection has to be Nancy, there is no other explanation.

I get the documents sorted at breakneck speed, print them out and leave them on Max's desk. Now to find out what my mother's been up to.

I'm gobsmacked when I open the messages. Alma is demanding money off Max, large amounts too. In one text she's asking for ten thousand pounds. Did he pay her? Tara told me about the woman at the door with *Alma* tattooed on her knuckles. Perhaps Max had been holding out on her and she had come here to collect.

He must have known about her and Nancy, or Alice, as the family knew her. Did Alma tell him they were sisters? If not, then how did she explain herself? But all that is secondary to the reason Alma could blackmail him in the first place. So she told him Alice was really Nancy, but that's no big deal. Was he trying to protect Nancy in some way? I'm clueless on that one too. Or was it just pure greed? Alma finds out Nancy is working here, makes up some imaginary dirt about her and threatens to spread the word. Max wouldn't like that; his whiter-than-white PA mixed up in some scandal or other, true or not. Alma was always good at making stuff up but I can't believe Max would fall for her lies. She's good but she drinks so much that she forgets and gets things mixed up. A man like him would see right through her.

Alma sent Max six texts in total, but he only replied to three of them. His replies were all the same: a big fat *no*. Alma's texts demanded money, no proper reason, just the words *I know what you did.*

What did he do? I ask myself. I wish I knew if this has anything to do with what's on the memory stick Nancy left for me too. I won't go anywhere near Alma, so I'll have to pluck up the courage and ask Max. But not yet. I want to know about Hanna first and to reassure myself that she's okay. Apart from that, Hanna told me that she had Nancy's box, and I certainly need to get my hands on that.

I decide to go for a walk. It's only early afternoon, the sun is shining and I could do with the fresh air. I grab my jacket and bag, lock my rooms and go downstairs. I should tell Tara where I'm going but she's comatose on the sofa.

I've not had a look round the village yet, and I need some time to clear my head. I have so many questions, but I don't seem to have a single answer. Yet.

. . .

It takes only minutes to reach the village. I've not seen it before, and it is a pretty little place, just like Hanna said. It's like stepping into a time gone by with its small shops and cobbled roads. There's even a village green with a duck pond at the centre. It's an idyllic place to live; Max and Tara are lucky to have all this on their doorstep. The park is just as picturesque, a mix of flower beds, manicured lawns and a neat children's playground. It's tucked to one side next to a large Victorian greenhouse.

I sit at a table outside in the sunshine and bask in the warmth. It's peaceful here; the only sound is that of the odd vehicle on the high street. I feel the sun on my face, close my eyes and go over the events of the past few days in my mind.

Things at the Marsden house are definitely not normal. Hanna is missing and no one is talking about it or about Isabel's visit on the night Hanna disappeared. I asked Max but all he told me was that she was okay. Meanwhile, Tara has checked out and Max has given me the key to his safe. It's all so confusing, as if I don't have enough mystery in my life.

Even though Hanna has a habit of creeping up on me and invading my space when I don't want her to, if she were to plonk herself beside me now, I'd be so relieved, I'd hug her. I have a bad feeling about her that I can't shift. I really hope that it's just my over-active imagination but I can't rid myself of the feeling that she's in danger.

'You need to be careful, you know how the sun brings out the freckles on your face, a drawback of having all that red hair.'

The sound of that voice makes me shudder. There is just so much I can cope with at any one time, and this is one nightmare too far. I can't describe how I feel, but shocked doesn't cover it.

'Come on, Alice, haven't you got anything to say to your old mother? It's been a while, you must have missed me?'

THIRTY

No, I damn well haven't. In fact, when I left home, I never wanted to see her evil face ever again, and that hasn't changed. But I can't sit here in silence, I have to say something, make her believe that I'm not at all bothered by her sudden appearance. But I am, the woman terrifies me. I wish it was different; as a child I prayed that she'd change, that she'd love me, but she never did. I don't know why she's like she is, I never did her any harm. I was a quiet child, Nancy told me I was no trouble at all, so why all the shouting, telling me how bad I was and how I'd never amount to anything.

The nerves, the need to run, to put as far as possible between me and her, mustn't show. If she suspects for a moment that I'm affected by her being her then I'm lost. She is the one person in this world who could always get the better of me.

'What are you up to?' I ask her, my face totally neutral. 'Apart from blackmailing Max Marsden, that is. You need to be careful,' I warn her. 'He's not the mild-mannered man he pretends to be.'

'Puts on a good act to the contrary though, doesn't he? I

think we both know what he really is. But what he hasn't grasped yet is that I'm ten times worse. You should tell him, make sure he knows who he's up against. If he values the comfortable world he lives in, he'll watch his step and stop accusing me of things I haven't done, like blackmail. If he doesn't stop, I have enough on him that the Marsden name will be dragged through the mud, and he'll find himself in a prison cell. How d'you think he'd cope with that?'

She has to be joking. No way can my twisted witch of a mother have anything on Max. They're strangers, their paths can't have crossed.

'What do you have on him, what's he done that's so dreadful that it brings you calling?'

'That's not something I want to talk about right now. But if he doesn't stop pointing the finger my way, I won't hold back. Social media is wonderful, don't you think? A few taps on a mobile and the whole world knows your business and the evil you've done.'

God, I hope she doesn't. Whether what she posts is true or not it's bound to have a bad effect on both Max and particularly Tara. Anyway, Alma's got no room to talk. Her past antics would make far better reading than anything Max has been up to.

'This must have something to do with Nancy; she's the only link between you and him.'

My mother smiles and raises those thick grey eyebrows of hers.

'Nancy was no angel despite what you think. If she was still alive, I might get my claws into her too.'

'Nancy was a good woman; she did no harm to anyone. She was the only one of my family I was fond of. I certainly never had any love for you.'

'Nor I for you or her,' she sneers. 'Nancy could be evil when she chose to be, she was clever too. Listen up, Alice, and

I'll tell you a little story, then we'll see if you're still so fond of Nancy.'

'Do your worst; whatever you say won't change a thing. I loved her and I always will.'

'A long time ago Nancy gave birth to a child. Afterwards she was ill with all that post-natal depression stuff and had to spend time in hospital. I was left with the screaming brat around my neck, and I swear she was even worse than you were.'

I have a vague memory of that time. I don't recall the child but I do remember the present I bought for it. I scraped together every last penny I had and bought the pretty pink blanket with the silk teddy in one corner.

I nod. 'The infant was put up for adoption.'

'Except that she wasn't.'

For one moment I think she's going to tell me something awful, that she'd become ill, perhaps even died, but she didn't; what comes next is almost as bad.

'There was no adoption, Alice. Nancy's infant daughter was sold.'

I can't begin to think what went on in the head of the woman sat in front of me. 'Nancy was away for months, and you're telling me that during that time, you sold her child?'

'She knew about it. I visited her in that place they put her in and explained.'

'That place they put her in, as you describe it, was a nursing home where she could recover.'

'Don't you want to know how much for and who to?'

She has that wild look on her face, the one she had when she leathered me for some imagined misdemeanour or other.

'The how much you can keep to yourself, I'm not interested.'

'But I bet who she went to is burning a hole in your brain.'

She's not wrong. Somewhere out there I have a cousin I've

never met, a blood relative who, with luck, will be like Nancy, someone I can get on with.

'Come on, Alice, ask the question. You're dying to know. I can see it on your face.'

She's right, I can't walk away without finding out the truth. 'Okay, what happened to her?'

'Nancy's infant daughter was sold to Max Marsden.'

THIRTY-ONE

I want to cry. This can't be true, people don't buy and sell a child. That would be heartbreaking. This has to be some wild scam Alma has dreamt up to extort money from Max. But there is a niggle in my mind. I remember the baby, and I remember Nancy being in hospital. Even as a young teenager, that bothered me. I'd hear Alma shouting at night when the baby cried. She showed the poor mite as much affection as she showed me, which was none at all.

I feel tears well up behind my eyes and turn away, I won't let Alma see me weep. I've never known what happened to Nancy's child; when she came out of hospital I'd already left home. I wrote to Nancy once and asked about the child, but she never replied. At the time that hurt, but if there is any truth in what Alma has told me, knowing Nancy back then, she'd wouldn't want to discuss it for fear of my mother's temper.

'You're lying, you have no proof of any of this.'

'I can see from your face that you know it's the truth. Whether you choose to accept it or not, Nancy sold her baby.'

'No, she didn't,' I sob. I can't help it, this is raw and too sad for me to just sit here and not react.

'Get a grip and dry your eyes, you always were an emotional fool.'

'Emotions... pity you don't have any. If you'd had an ounce of decency, my life and Nancy's would have been very different.'

'I arranged things, I was there, Marsden gave me the money and I handed the brat over. No fuss, few words and I was rid of the responsibility. I visited Nancy and made her see reason. Convinced her that she would never have coped.'

'Why would Max and Tara have to resort to that anyway. I'm sure they must be able to have their own children, they're both young and healthy.'

Alma says nothing in reply but sits opposite me tutting. The woman I remember was evil and, despite it being years since I last had anything to do with her, she hasn't changed a bit.

'I am telling you the truth, Alice. What reason do I have to lie to you?'

'Blackmail is a good enough reason, so don't come play the innocent with me.'

'You're wrong; I am not blackmailing anyone.'

'Come on then, tell me the story.' I sit back, arms folded and wait for the fairy tale to begin.

'Marsden's wife couldn't have children, and it made her go mad in the head. Back then she had a drink problem too. They were refused by every adoption agency they approached. She was desperate for a child, so he, silly bugger, bought one for her.'

'That's why you're blackmailing him? You're making money out of their pain and misery?'

'Not me, love, but I reckon someone is and it serves him right. He only did it for her, to stop her whining and making herself ill. But look at the aggro it's brought him; he'd have been better off ditching her and finding someone else.'

'It was you who organised this. Nancy was in hospital and I bet she knew nothing about it.'

'The details don't concern you, just know that it was sorted and a sum agreed.'

The woman has no soul. How can she sell her sister's infant and feel no guilt? 'If Max paid you back then, why chase him for more now?'

Alma shields her eyes from the bright sunshine as she looks at me.

'I want nothing from the man. The problem is he thinks I do. And that's what I'm doing here, to set the record straight.'

That's a first. But if she's not blackmailing Max, then who is?

'You could do me a favour, Alice. You can tell Marsden to stop giving me grief. The man is unhinged. I know the type, capable of anything. Once I've put him straight, I'll be out of here fast.'

I'm juggling information, trying to put what I know into some sort of order. I'm confident that Nancy played no part in the sale of her child or blackmailing Max. Despite all her protestations of innocence, that just leaves Alma. She has to be the blackmailer.

Blackmailer or not, there is another more important thing to consider. The baby sold to Max has to be Hanna.

Hanna is Nancy's child. I can't believe it, but it makes sense why Nancy took the job with the Marsdens. Does Hanna know, if not should I be the one to tell her?

Alma has turned up out of the blue and done what she always does: cause mayhem. This can of worms will take some containing, and I shouldn't be the one to take on that task.

'My advice is to go home, crawl back under whatever rock you came out from, and never ever come back. If I see you again it'll be far too soon. You've done enough damage to last the Marsden family a lifetime.'

She seems to have taken that little mouthful well. She shrugs her shoulders, sips on her coffee and gives me a smile.

'Okay, let's leave all talk of Marsden for now and talk about you, my beloved daughter,' she says with a sneer. 'You can start with where you've been hiding all these years.'

'None of your business.'

'I'm surprised you're still alive, if I'm honest. I did hear that you'd crossed that loan shark, Andrew Wolfenden, and you know what happens to those poor buggers. Does he know where you are now, that you've got yourself a cushy number in the sticks?'

'You don't know what you're talking about. And Andrew Wolfenden has more important things to worry about these days than chasing me. Last I heard, he's ill and living abroad.'

'Lucky you.' She laughs. 'No more Wolf, but one of his cronies will have taken over. Mark my words, girl, you'd better watch your step or one of these dark nights you'll cop for it.'

Nice, I don't see my mother for years and when I do she wants me dead. If this is the sort of parent I was spawned from, it's no wonder I ran away.

'Donna?'

It's Nicco. I hadn't even seen him walking up to our table, yet here he is, standing next to us, blocking out the sun.

'D'you know this woman?'

Do I tell him the truth – that she's my disaster of a mother – or do I lie and tell him she's an acquaintance? But the decision is taken out of my hands when, before I get a chance to respond, Alma pipes up.

'We're mother and daughter,' she purrs at him. 'We haven't seen each other for several years and are having a catch-up, so if whatever you want is not life-threatening, then I suggest you get lost.'

I wince. There's no need to be rude, but that's Alma all over. Still, I'm surprised she spoke to Nicco like that, given he looks like a prize fighter.

'Sorry to disturb.' He gives a little bow. 'Catch you later, Donna.'

He took that well, but still, the whole interaction has put me on edge. I watch him disappear onto the high street and find myself wishing he'd come back. I need rescuing, and Nicco is a more than able candidate.

'So, you go by *Donna* now, do you? Why's that? Running away from something? Got something to hide? Does lover boy over there even know the real you?'

'Look, Alma, I've had enough of your company, so why don't you go and get on with whatever you're here for,' I tell her, avoiding the question.

'I'm your mother, so don't address me by my name; it's not right.'

'You don't deserve to be called *mother*, so don't start,' I retaliate. 'Alma is as good as it's ever going to get, so live with it.'

It strikes me that Hanna and I have that in common and for the same reasons. We both refuse to acknowledge our parents are just that.

'Have it your way but this is a long way from over. Your new boss has made a big mistake.'

'Max can look after himself.'

'They have a daughter. What is she now? Twenty-three by my reckoning...'

'How's that relevant? Hanna has nothing to do with you.'

'Hanna, as you call her, is at the heart of this. You do know that isn't her real name, the name she was registered with at birth?'

No, I didn't, but I suppose it stands to reason that Max will have changed it.

'What is her name?'

'I'm not telling you. You reckon you're so clever, find out for yourself.'

I leave the table and my disaster of a mother and walk away.

So much for my quiet time in the sunshine. The afternoon has been a nightmare and I wish I hadn't bothered.

As I walk, I go over what Alma told me. I can't believe that Max bought Hanna when she was an infant, but it would solve the mystery of why Nancy came here. She simply wanted to find her daughter. What I don't know is did Nancy ever tell Hanna who she really was. Hanna has not said or even hinted that Nancy was anything other than her father's PA and a friend to her.

I don't believe all that rubbish Alma told me about why she's here. My head is so full of stuff I'm trying to process that I didn't ask Alma the obvious question: if she's not blackmailing Max, what's she doing here? I don't believe that putting-the-record-straight nonsense. Alma doesn't give a damn about such stuff.

If she'd come to Nancy's funeral, I could understand it, but she didn't. Is it possible that Nancy was helping Alma? Feeding her information about Max?

I can't believe that Nancy would be party to blackmail but Hanna did say she had money. From what I remember, she was as skint as the rest of us, so what changed?

The house is noisy when I return, but there is no sign of Hanna or Tara.

I hear loud music coming from the office. It's Max with the radio turned up full blast. He sees me and gestures for me to come in. Another invite into Max's sanctum, I'm honoured.

He seems very jolly, almost overpoweringly so. It strikes me he's a man pretending all is well when it certainly isn't. He might not fool anyone else who knows his recent history but he appears to have convinced himself. He's all smiles, casually dressed in jeans and t-shirt and humming to himself.

'Earworm,' he explains. 'The song played in the pub for

most of last night and now I can't get it out of my head. Lock in,' he whispers. 'Just what I needed, a skinful. He's a real mate is Keith, the landlord.'

I say nothing. How can he just go off to the pub, get drunk and leave Tara in that state and with Hanna missing? This is one odd family. I don't understand them, but do I really want to? Sort the Nancy thing and get out of here, that was always my plan and I should stick to it.

'I'm pleased you've settled in, Donna. It calms the nerves to know that I have someone I can trust in my life, and that my business is in safe hands.'

I can't believe he's just said that. Safe hands is a long way from what I am. I'm fumbling my way around at best. Just as I'm about to say something, the office phone rings and he picks up the receiver.

'Donna. Did you want something?' he asks sternly.

So much for conversation, I've been dropped like a hot brick. Whoever he's speaking to obviously has priority.

'Your passport is on your desk and I've almost finished the documents you wanted.'

He smiles and then nods. It's time for me to go to my rooms.

THIRTY-TWO

'I'm busy, Donna. What is it?'

He's irritated by my appearance and I don't understand why. This is a swift mood change; this is a different man from the jolly Max of only thirty minutes ago. I hand him the sheets. 'I didn't mean to disturb, but I've finished and wanted to catch you.'

His eyes scan the sheets, then he hands them back.

'I'm afraid these won't do. The formatting's all wrong. I want double line spacing and the text centred on the page.'

Shame he didn't tell me. Instructions given, he slams the door in my face. This version of Max doesn't appeal at all. Where is the pleasant man who only ten minutes ago was as happy as Larry and praising my work?

As I was told, I alter the text and reprint. Gathering the sheets, I walk along to Max's office for a second time. He's not here, and this time the door is locked. What am I supposed to do with these? There's no Tara to give them to. I'll dump them on the hall table; he's bound to check there, even if it's to leave his phone. There is a pile of post on the table; before I finish for the day I'd better check there's nothing important.

There are bills, advertising junk and a request for a brochure, nothing of any note. That is until I spot the one addressed to Nancy Williams.

Leaving the other stuff, I grasp the letter and hurry back to my rooms. I still haven't got the one I reckon is hidden in Nancy's box. Hanna was supposed to give it to me before events made that impossible.

Tearing at the envelope, I take out a single sheet of paper. There is no sender's address and no signature at the bottom. In the centre of the sheet are the words:

You let me down.

Whoever sent this knows Nancy's real name but I've no idea who sent it or what it means. It could be from Alma, but this isn't her style. If she wanted to tell Nancy something she'd say it in person. This is another mystery I can do without. It seems logical to suspect this is from the same person who sent the first letter, which means I need to get my hands on the box.

The house is deathly quiet as I tiptoe along the corridor. There's no sign of Max. For once I'm in luck, and it's about time I had some. I thank God that he didn't pick up the post either. I can't imagine what he would have made of the one meant for Nancy.

The smell of meat roasting is wafting through the house. Maria is making dinner, and, at some point, Tara and Max are going to head down to the dining room, so I have to do what I'm about to do quickly.

Hanna's bedroom door is unlocked. I know she won't mind, but I still feel like a thief. If I'm caught by Max or Tara, I'll be in trouble. Admit what I'm here for, and I'll never get my hands on the damn box. Hanna has left it on her dressing table in front of the window. She did get it for me, good girl. I grab it and run.

Back in my rooms I try to remember the sequence of moves that open the drawer. Nancy made it look so easy. She used to put jewellery in it and photos underneath. I hope she took them out, there's no way I want to see those faces again.

Lift the lid, move the small knob on the drawer to the right and pull. Fat lot of good remembering does me, age and dirt have made the hinges stiff. As much as I try I can't budge the thing. What I really need is a hammer and chisel.

'Donna, come down here!'

It's Max. What a moment to choose to call me; it's almost as if he knows what I'm up to. His tone doesn't sound friendly either. So much for the happy Max I spoke to earlier. It sounds as if I'm in for an ear-bashing, so I put the box aside and leave Hanna's room quietly.

I hurry down the stairs to find him waiting in the hall, the stupid printouts in his hand.

'These are still not satisfactory, I'm afraid, Donna.'

This is deliberate; he's using the printouts as a way to wear me down. Well, two can play that game.

'Is this a wind-up?' I demand angrily. 'Are you playing some weird game?'

Now he looks surprised. It strikes me that I wasn't supposed to answer back but meekly take the sheets and scuttle off to my office. Well, stuff that.

'There's nothing wrong with them, and you know it.' My voice is sharp, my gaze unwavering as I face him. I'm pissed off and it shows; boss or not, he can't do this and expect to get away with it.

'Wind-up? How dare you speak to me in that tone. I'm your boss. You need to learn how to behave. Keep up this insolent attitude of yours and you will go the same way as Hanna.'

What does he mean by that? Does he know where she is? And is he threatening me? 'Where is Hanna? If either you or Tara has harmed her, I'll go to the police.'

'The police,' he mocks. 'You'd never be believed. I have influence, the chief constable is a friend, we play golf together most weekends, and you're a nobody. No one in their right mind would believe you over me.'

'Perhaps not, but if I tell them about a missing daughter whose family are not interested in finding her, they might take notice. Even if they don't, add in what you did to her bedroom, and the gossip would make good listening. People have a habit of remembering such things; some of them, particularly the papers, like to dig deep. Who knows what they might turn up.' I smile.

The look on his face suggests he's no idea what I'm talking about. He waves the sheets in front of my face. 'I asked for a larger character size.'

'No, you didn't.' I'm not deaf or stupid. I remember very well what he asked for.

'You are getting close to pushing me too far, Donna, and that's not a good idea.'

This is another attempt to frighten me. What Max doesn't realise is when people piss me off to the degree that he has, the urge to fight back is strong. The life I've led has toughened me up and when necessary made me a formidable enemy.

'Nice try, Max, but you're dealing with the wrong person. You and Tara have been kind to me and I'm grateful to you both, so I'll cut you some slack. But know this: I can be every bit as scary as you. More so if I ask for help from the scum I knew before I came here.'

His eyes are pinpoints and his face red with rage. He wants to lash out but isn't sure what my reaction will be. I'll give him a clue.

'I'm not Hanna, you can't bully me and get away with it. I will fight back, and you will lose. Back off, apologise, and I'll let you off with this warning.'

Too far, perhaps, but I was impressive, even if I say so myself.

'This isn't the end. You will not get the better of me,' he retaliates.

'I think I already have. So far you've seen the nice Donna, the one with manners and gratitude, but I have another side, one that can easily sort you if pushed. I won't listen to any more nonsense about these bloody sheets. I'm close to ripping them to bits and stuffing them down your throat.'

'I dare you, insolent bitch.'

He's resorted to name-calling now, not that I give a damn. I've been called much, much worse.

'Be a good girl, go back to your office and this time do your job. This is your last chance, Donna, get them wrong again and I'll punish you.'

I'm beginning to wonder if he's actually mad. *Punish*, is that what happened to Hanna, after she spoke to Isabel the way she did? If so then poor Hanna will have been terrified.

I'm having difficulty with this. Max appears to have some sort of mental switch, flick it and this controlling bully emerges. This version of Max is miles away from the one I met at the funeral.

'Where is Hanna?' I demand. 'What have you done to her? And don't pretend otherwise... we saw you lead her away and she hasn't been seen since.'

'I've no idea where Hanna is. We did go outside; I wanted her to cool down, come to her senses, but she ran off towards the road and hasn't been home or contacted us.'

'I don't believe you. I've seen for myself how vindictive you can be.'

'I'm not lying, Donna. Hanna has disappeared and we don't know what's happened to her. She has none of her things either, no cash card or mobile. Both Tara and I are worried sick. I've rung round and asked everyone I can think of if they've seen her. I even went round the shops in the village. I've no idea what to do next; the girl is breaking our hearts.'

How do I react to this? Max has just given me a right going-over about some stupid printouts, now he wants sympathy. My head is spinning; for the life of me I can't work out who the good guy is in this house and who's bluffing.

'Are you sure you've tried everywhere? Is there a friend Hanna could have gone to, perhaps?'

'She has no one close who'd likely take her in. You've not been here long but you must have noticed how insular she is. Hanna doesn't seem to need anyone, not even me or Tara these days.'

'I don't think we should wait, just hope she'll suddenly turn up; anything could happen to her. When I get back to my office I'll ring the police, report her missing.'

'No, not yet, Tara won't like it. She won't like the public and probably press attention our missing daughter would attract.'

Attention, is that all he's worried about? The more attention, the better, in my opinion. But Max has flicked that mood switch again; he's behaving better, more like a caring parent.

This is insane. Their behaviour is driving me up the wall. The sooner I get out of here, the better, but first I'm going to make sure Hanna is safe.

THIRTY-THREE

The following morning, I wander into the kitchen looking for some breakfast; Maria tells me that Max has been delayed because his accountant wants to see him urgently. He's taking a later flight and has left me a list of emails he wants sending.

A bowl of cereal and a mug of coffee later, I risk the sitting room and a possible encounter with Tara. For now, I have to keep the peace and not rock the boat if I'm to get to the bottom of what's going on. Really, what I want to do is give her a shake, a good slapping, and tell her to find her daughter.

I find her sitting on the sofa, calm and her usual beautiful self: perfect hair, make-up done. She has a visitor: Nicco.

'I've been telling Nicco about Max's awful behaviour.' Tara smiles at me, completely ignoring the fact that hers can be equally bad. 'The thing with the documents he wanted for today is an example of Max being stressed. He's always like this when he's working too hard.'

I'd love to tell her how I really feel, about her, Max, this whole family, but it would only stir things up if I air what I felt.

'The man's a psychopath,' Nicco says with meaning.

Psychopath, that's some accusation, but I can see where he's coming from. I would stick that description on Tara too, but perhaps with her it's this problem she has with moods, depression and swallowing peppermints instead of pills that makes her behaviour erratic.

I am surprised that this pair are so open with each other; I'd no idea they were even close. They are both saying it as it is with Max, and I'm not sure how to respond. Listening to them makes me uncomfortable, if I'm honest. I work here and don't want to join in a conversation pulling a family member apart, even if it is about Max.

'He's under pressure, he gets moody, but it doesn't last,' she says.

'That's not strictly true,' Nicco warns. 'Max is two-faced; he acts the part of a nice guy who understands and wants to help, but the truth is he hasn't got a sensitive bone in his body. My advice is don't rile him,' he tells me. 'Max is unpredictable, push him too far and he explodes in a fit of temper. I don't want either of you harmed. When things get tough, remember you have my card, Donna; it has my mobile number on it. Feel free to ring me at any time, and I mean that.'

Tara looks miserable. All this talk about her husband's failings isn't doing her any good.

'This isn't pleasant for you, Donna, but please don't leave us. There's nothing I can do about Max right now, but he will apologise for all his bad behaviour, I'm sure of it.'

I won't hold my breath. Max's behaviour is getting worse. In my opinion he's capable of anything. Nicco's description of him is spot on.

'I've no intention of leaving yet, Tara.' I nod. 'For the time being, I need the job.'

A job, yes; involvement in this mess, no.

She pats my hand and smiles. 'Thanks, knowing you're in the house means a lot to me.'

Yesterday I had Mad Max to deal with, and now this.

'Max knows he can't get the better of you, Donna. You took him on at the restaurant and won. Hanna told me all about it. You've no idea what a boost that gave me.'

Here we go, Tara's admitted she needs me; in that case, I'll say my piece.

'I've seen for myself what Max is like, and I don't like it any more than you do, but you can't sit back and ignore what could have happened to Hanna. He is the last person Hanna was seen with. It's possible he's harmed her, that she needs help, we should do something.'

Tara turns on the tears; it ruins her carefully applied eye make-up, and now her perfectly applied black mascara is running down her cheeks.

'Max told me to wait, to do nothing because he has everything in hand. I daren't cross him, Donna; he'll get so angry and that won't do any of us any good. He said I was to take no notice of you either, that you are a bad influence on Hanna.'

'Do you do everything Max tells you?'

'The alternative is hard to take for both me and Hanna.'

'Psychopath,' Nicco says again, and I have to agree with him. But what to do about it? Tara is on a knife edge; she can't take much more of Max and his cruelty. She doesn't want me and him to have a blazing row either. A change of subject, I think.

'You answered the door to a woman with a name tattooed on her knuckles. Have you seen her since?'

This is the sort of chaos my mother thrives on, and despite her protests to the contrary, I know she's trying to blackmail Max; given the circumstances, it's exactly what she would do. I smile to myself; Max should learn that any contact with my mother does no one any good.

'I've glimpsed her once since then, two days ago in the village,' Tara says.

Alma has no friends round here but must be staying somewhere, a bed and breakfast place, perhaps.

'Is this woman important?' Nicco asks, turning to Tara.

'I've no idea; she asked for Max, so I presumed he must know her.'

'Did you tell him that she came here to the house?'

'Yes, and he went into one of his moods, locked himself in his office and drank half a bottle of whisky.'

'Are you sure you have no idea where Hanna is, Tara?' I try again. 'If you know anything at all, no matter how unimportant you think it is, you must speak up.'

'I've no idea where she is, and that's the truth.'

I know her well enough to know the innocent look on her face is a sham. Despite her protestations, she's lying, and I feel sure that she does know something.

'Tell her,' Nicco says finally. 'You need to make her aware of what Max is capable of.'

'She has been missing before because Max had locked her up,' Tara admits. 'But only when she was out of control. It was always in her old bedroom, but I've checked and she's not there.'

That's no excuse, and I'm surprised Hanna never told me.

'Is there somewhere else he might put her?' I ask, dreading her answer, given Nicco believes the man to be unhinged.

'In the pig shed, chained up so she can't escape.'

THIRTY-FOUR

The pig shed, I should have guessed. Hanna might do the feeding and the mucking out but under duress. She told me that she hates the things and that they terrify her. The poor woman must be going through hell.

Before another word is said, I leave the sitting room and make for the kitchen. 'Maria, are there any spare wellies I can borrow?'

'Yes, there are some in the cupboard in the utility room.'

She doesn't even look up from what she's doing, and simply carries on stacking the dishwasher. I rush into the utility room and I flick off my trainers before stepping into a pair that look about my size.

Hanna is not staying in that hell-hole any longer. Max won't get away with this; I'll talk to Hanna, get her to make a complaint. False imprisonment is what it is, and that's against the law.

I race across the lawn and, breathless, stand looking at the scene in front of me. The pig shed door is closed but the pigs are going in and out through the flap at the bottom, like a cat flap only much bigger.

I'm nervous, I don't want to go in there, but I need to get Hanna free so I've no choice. I can't stand and watch the animals root around in the mud all afternoon.

The wellies are just the job, but like the shoes I wore on that first day, they're too big, and I'm slithering my way across the mud and heaven knows what else. I'm within an arm's-length of the door when everything changes. I hear squelching noises behind me, but before I can turn to see who it is, I feel a heavy blow to the back of my head and everything around me fades to nothing.

* * *

When I come round, everything around me is dark, cold and stinks. I've no idea how much time has passed. I have a blinding headache but I'm more focused on the gut-wrenching stench of the pigs. Seconds later I throw up. I have pigs around my feet and scream at them between coughing and spitting vomit out of my mouth.

It has to be Max who hit me and dragged me in here. It can't have been Tara or Nicco; they were still in the sitting room when I left, and Hanna is still missing. I know Max hasn't left for Spain yet, so who else can it be? When he does leave, he'll be gone a couple of days, and there is no way I can be in here for that long. I hate to admit it, but right now Max has me beaten. I stand little chance of getting out of this one but that doesn't mean I'm not going to try. And when I do, Max Marsden will pay dearly for what he's done to me.

Fighting talk, but realistically, that's all it is. I've been attacked and imprisoned in this dreadful place. I've left my mobile in the bedroom, so I can't call for help, and there isn't much chance of escape either. I'm chained to one of the supporting posts. The chain has a manacle attached to the end and my right wrist is locked into it. Without a key to get the thing off, escape is impossible. My fate is with the gods, and I don't like it, not one bit.

I've felt like this once before on a cold night spent shivering on the icy floor of a shop doorway. On that occasion, fear and hopelessness gave way to fight and anger. I hope I've still got some of that resilience left in me. Where that fight will come from, I don't know; right now I feel like shit and can barely stand up. I'm tired, mentally exhausted and fit only for sleep.

I'm chained up next to a stack of straw bales. The chain is long enough that I can pull one from the top of the pile to sit on. I flop down with my aching head leaning against the wooden post.

It's still dark outside but moonlight filters through the gaps in the wooden slats, casting shadows all over the shed. It allows me to see a little of what's happening in here. Pigs, basically, and not much else. They are spread out over the floor, lying down and grunting. The noise is like someone in bed with their mouth open and snoring their head off. One, huge and covered in mud and worse, is leaning hard against my leg. I kick out with the other one, and with a squeal and a flurry of trotters, it moves away.

My situation is dire; it would be so easy to give up, go back to sleep and hope help isn't too long in coming. But that's not my style. There are a couple of plus points. Only one of my hands is manacled to the chain, and the pig flap is large enough for me to crawl through. The manacle is where I'll start; one way or another it has to come off.

I forget sleep and my aching head for the moment; I'm determined not to give up. I'm strong when I need to be. I will tug and tug until the post falls down if I have to.

I thank God that I'm at my lowest weight because I reckon that if I work at it, twist and pull at the manacle, it could slip right off my wrist. I can freely turn it round on my wrist, so I should be in with a chance.

Time ticks by. This isn't working; the manacle won't budge. I want to close my eyes, drift off into oblivion. The pigs aren't sleeping anymore; I can see them moving about, hear them grunt and snuffle.

The huge thing that I kicked away before is back, and he's brought a friend with him. They are both snuffling around my feet, and then the pair bed down again beside me. I close my eyes; I don't want to look at them. I can't bear the thought of what they might do once I'm dead. I know pigs will eat anything, they have strong jaws; I don't fancy becoming a rare treat for this pair.

I still haven't found Hanna, but if she is in here, she must be terrified. My opinion of her has fluctuated during my time here, but on balance, she's okay. Now I know she's my cousin, that is if Alma is to be believed, so I'm more inclined to understand how she is. I reckon the spitefulness is a reaction to how Max has treated her.

I call out her name but get no reply. I pray that she's not lying somewhere in this hell-hole, unconscious and at the mercy of these dreadful creatures. I call out again, but there's still silence. My one priority is to find her.

The pigs are suddenly taking more interest in me than is comfortable. More of them have left the pen and come back inside. There's also a rustling in one of the bales beside me. I've heard a noise like that before, and it makes me go cold. Nightfall hasn't just brought the pigs inside; it's woken up the rats too. Like the pigs, they're another of nature's creatures I can do without. I saw enough of them when I stayed with Ella. Her bedsit was in the cellar; at night they appeared looking for food, and they were rarely disappointed. Ella's staple diet is take-aways, curry, pizza, anything that comes in a carton and doesn't require effort. She isn't the tidiest or most hygienic of people either. At times, empty cartons littered the place and the rats had a field day. Ella got used to them, she had no fear at all, but not me. Tolerate at a pinch, but used to? Never. I now know what the rustling was in the night – a rat slunk by right in front of me. I'm not daft, where you get one rat there are others not far away.

I can't stay here for much longer but I have to put my own situation aside for now, Hanna desperately needs my help. I tug at the manacle, twisting and turning my fingers, but it achieves nothing. If I had something like soap and water or oil to make my hand slippery, I might get somewhere, but there's no chance of that in here. However, there is something that might work.

Gross and sick-making as it is, I can use mud and pig mess to smooth the way. Bending down, I scoop up a handful of the stuff. Not pleasant, but I have no choice. Give up, don't give it a go, and I'm as good as dead. I spread the goo liberally over my manacled hand and wrist while doing my best not to choke on vomit. This has to work; if it doesn't, I'm all out of ideas.

Holding the manacle with my free hand, I desperately try to work my fingers through the hoop of steel. I've bent my thumb into my palm and have my fingers bunched together. With my thin hands, this shouldn't be so damned hard. More tugging and twisting the thing with my free hand, but still no joy. If I'm not careful I'm in danger of breaking my wrist. Even so, I'm not giving up. I get free, and a broken wrist is worth the pain.

It takes what seems an eternity but finally my hand moves. I slaver on more pig mess and try again. Another tug and my hand is free, leaving me breathless and the manacle swinging empty from the chain.

Picking up a handful of straw, I do the best I can to clean up my wrist and hand. A good effort, but not like soap and water. What I'd give now for a hot bath and a stiff drink.

The pig flap idea works too. I wriggle through it easily and stand for a moment in the pig pen. It's pouring with rain, not a hot bath but very welcome. I stand for several minutes with my head facing the sky and my arms outstretched, palms up. The rain will wash a little of the muck off, freshen me up and help me feel less tired.

Getting out of that horror is all very well, but Hanna still needs my help. It's not fully light yet and I have to be careful where I put my feet, but that doesn't stop me picking my way fast across the muddy floor of the pen towards the gate. There is a huge pig lying against it, and there's no chance of me shoving it out of the way. It's grunting, twitching its ears while it stares at me. It makes me shudder; it'd suit me if I don't see another pig ever again.

I fix my eyes on the ground as I shuffle past; if I'd been looking anywhere else, I'd have missed it. Lying in the mud with tattered skin hanging onto bone is a human hand.

I'm terrified that it might belong to Hanna.

All sorts of stuff runs through my head. Top of the list: is Hanna dead? That thought makes me weep, and I throw up, I can't help it. I've spent the night in a filthy pig shed, I'm probably still concussed from the bash on the head, and the young woman I've just found out is my cousin might have been murdered. I can't take much more. The sooner I find Hanna and leave this house and the people in it, the better.

Wiping vomit from my mouth with the sleeve of my blouse, I bend down for a closer look. I have to make sure it is a human hand. But I'm not wrong, it's human alright, but there is only one finger complete, and it's impossible to work out which it is.

I almost faint when I see what's tattooed on the knuckle: the capital letter A.

THIRTY-FIVE

I have to be in shock; no one could look at what I've just seen and not be. The A could be part of the name Hanna, and that terrifies me, but then I realise that Hanna does not have any tattoos. I'm not thinking right; that'll be down to my experience in the pig shed. That leaves just one option: the hand has to belong to Alma. She had the initials of her first name tattooed on the knuckles of her right hand. As much as I hated Alma for what she did to me in the past, she was still my mother, and this is not the end I would have wished for her.

It can only be Max who murdered her. She called at the house once but that was a while ago. As far as I'm aware, no one else but Max knew who she was or even that she was staying in the village. Knowing Max's erratic moods and temper, it has to be him, no one else has a motive.

I have to find Hanna before something awful happens to her. It looks as if Max has killed once, and the last thing I want is for Hanna to become another of his victims.

I've checked her old bedroom and I know she's not in the pig shed. I'll search the house, check every room to make sure she's not been locked in or is so afraid she's hiding.

I enter the house through the back door. Thankfully, Maria isn't in the kitchen, and the hallway is empty too. There's no sound of voices or music playing, just deathly silence. I take the stairs with shivers sliding down my back. The atmosphere is all wrong.

I have to check that neither Max nor Tara is in their bedroom. The day is still early so it's possible they're not up yet. With my ear to the bedroom door, I hear the splash of water and the sound of Max singing to himself. He's in the shower.

I open the bedroom door and peek inside, no sign of Tara. I creep forward to the door of the en suite and hear Max humming to himself. This is not the confrontation I want. I'd prefer a face-to-face in the office or the sitting room, but it is what it is.

He's standing naked and soaking wet under the stream of hot water, no doubt convinced he's got rid of me. It's him who's going to get the shock. There's no time to tidy myself up now. I can't lose this chance; I've got just the break I need.

But I can't just take him on; he's killed once, so weedy little me won't give him a problem. There's a cabinet on the landing, full of books, no use for what I've got in mind, but on one of the shelves there's a large brass ornament of a cat. I tiptoe out and grab hold of the thing. It's large and heavy; the cat's tail curled over its back makes the perfect handle. One swing, one heavy blow to the head, and Max Marsden won't trouble anyone again. Now to give him the surprise of his life.

Pushing the bathroom door ajar, I see him. He's got his back to me and is reaching for a towel. I won't get a better chance than this. Don't freeze. I tell myself, no more nerves – you promised.

Each second I look at him seems like a lifetime. Only a few days ago I would have enjoyed seeing him like this. I had thought him handsome, I even fancied him, saw him as the perfect man and one I'd like for myself. How could I get it so wrong? Just shows how little experience I've had of men that I can't recognise a bastard when I meet one. Seeing him stood there naked, vulnerable, all I feel now is revulsion and hate.

I want an end to this for what he's done to me, Alma and possibly Hanna, but I need a good swing at his head. Impossible while he's stood up. But I have got the element of surprise, he's no idea I'm here and that gives me the upper hand. Hiding the cat behind my back I make my move.

One push of the bathroom door and I'm in. But Max sees me. He grabs a towel, wraps it around his waist, and seconds later is at my side.

'Donna, what's happened, you're covered in mud and smell to high heaven?'

'You know very well what happened,' I scream at him. The bathroom is hot, the air steamy. I sway on my feet, I'm about to fall to the ground when Max puts me on a chair.

'I've got you,' Max says. 'You'd better sit down.'

I have to stay focused. I have to confront him; I need to find Hanna.

'What have you done with Hanna?'

'Nothing at all; like you, I'm waiting for her to come home. The back of your head is bleeding, have you fallen?'

'No, someone clouted me in the pig pen,' I say, pushing him away. 'I think I was out of it for a few seconds, might have been longer.'

'You're probably concussed. I'll take you to A&E, get you looked at.'

'I'm not going anywhere with you, that would be stupid.' I gently touch the wound. 'You did this to me, and I know what you did to Alma, I've seen the proof for myself.'

He looks puzzled and shakes his head.

'I have no idea what you're talking about. You're not thinking straight.'

'That's where you're wrong.'

'I do think you should see a doctor, but if you won't, then you should go to your rooms, shower and then rest.'

'Do that and I'm a sitting duck; look what you did to Alma.'

'I'm sorry, Donna, but if you won't let me help you, there's nothing I can do.'

He sounds so sincere, so caring, but it's a front. Max Marsden is neither of those things. 'What I want you to do is leave me alone. I don't want your help; I want to find Hanna.'

'Okay, I'll back off. Clean yourself up, then get back to the office where you belong.'

'And Hanna, what have you done with her?'

'I've no idea where she's gone but I, for one, am enjoying the peace and quiet.'

Now we have it, a taste of the real Max, the one he tries unsuccessfully to keep under control. I'm angry; no, worse than that, I'm seething with bloody rage. How can he be so casual about Hanna's disappearance, with a mangled hand lying in the pig pen? Doesn't he understand that anything could have happened to his daughter? With one screaming roar, I swing the brass cat at his head.

But he dodges out of the way and grabs the thing off me.

'What is this about, Donna? Why are you hell-bent on killing me?'

'Because of what you did to me, because you murdered Alma and heaven knows what you've done to Hanna.'

I lost control, I should not have lashed out like that. I start to shake as reality kicks in. I can't be right in the head. I look at him and blink, I nearly killed the man. I came close to caving his head in. That's not me, that's not who I am.

I feel sick again and the ache at the back of my head is worse. I take one more look at Max, reach out to him in an effort to steady myself, then fall to the floor.

THIRTY-SIX

I come round on the sitting room sofa. Max is standing over me, talking to a man I don't recognise.

'This is Doctor Walsh,' Max tells me. 'You've had a nasty bang on the head and are mildly concussed.'

I don't stink any more; looking at my arms and legs, they are clean, and I'm wearing my dressing gown.

'Not down to me, Donna,' Max reassures me with one of those special smiles. 'Maria sorted you out.'

'Tell her thanks from me.'

'Take two of these in four hours,' the doctor tells me. 'They're for the headache. A good night's sleep and you'll be fine.'

I hope so, I can't do with feeling like this for much longer. Banging my head, feeling sick and then there's the collapsing in a heap at Max's feet. He must have loved that one.

The doctor leaves and it's just me and Max. I'm dreading what's coming next. I'm confused, he could have done me real harm when I was out of it, but he didn't. *Good Max, bad Max,* I wish he'd decide which one he's sticking with then I'll know how to deal with him.

'Why did you lock me in the pig shed?'

A simple enough question. He can't deny it; he's the only one who would do that. I can disregard Tara, Nicco and Hanna, so that just leaves him.

'I didn't, whatever you think, it wasn't down to me. I wouldn't do that to anyone.'

He's lying, Tara told me he's done the same to Hanna. 'But there isn't anyone else, and the pigs are your thing.'

'True, but I don't lock people in their shed.'

I don't want to believe him but he didn't harm me when he had the opportunity; he even called the doctor.

'For now I'll give you the benefit of the doubt, but what about Alma?'

'Who is Alma?'

He's at it again – *don't know, it wasn't me* – when I know damn well it wasn't anyone else. 'Don't even try to deny you do know her, Max. She came to this house, she asked for you, why would she do that if she's a complete stranger?'

'She might have been here for one of many reasons. I meet so many people, a lot of them because of my business. Who did she speak to?'

'Tara.'

'There you are then. Not guilty.' He smiles.

'Well, someone is because Alma's hand is rotting away in your pig pen.'

That stopped Max in his tracks. He's looking at me with worried eyes, guilt? It could be.

'You've seen it?'

'Yes, on my way out of the place. I know the hand is hers because her initial is tattooed on the knuckle of the remaining finger.'

I can see that worries him: the wrinkled forehead, the way he pulls his mouth into a straight line.

'You might not know this but pigs can be dangerous creatures. People who look after them have to take great care not to injure themselves or for any reason lose consciousness when they are with them.'

'Like me, you mean.'

'You had a lucky escape; being locked in the shed will have helped. The pigs have learned that it's for sleeping in and not eating.'

It takes a few seconds for the implications of that to register.

'Eating... you're not saying that pigs can actually eat people? That's insane.'

'Actually, it's not. Pigs are more than capable of eating a full-grown adult in a short space of time. They devour the lot, flesh, bone, even clothing. They have strong jaws.'

Something else that makes me wince and go cold. It'll be a while before I get the image it conjures out of my head.

'You're saying that's what happened to Alma?'

'It's a real possibility given what you saw. Leaving the hand was probably due to it being flung and landing wherever you found it.'

Hanna said a few things about the pigs but not that bit. Given her tendency to throw in the odd scary detail in the conversations we've had, I'm surprised.

'In that case, you should find the hand before it disappears down a pig's throat. It's evidence, and the police will want it.'

If he is innocent, he won't object, no sane person would. But this is Max, and I have real doubts about his mental state.

'You're right.' I'm relieved. 'If it's still there, I'll bag it up and call the police right away. And I'll get Tara and Maria to search the house for Hanna.'

That's a relief, it's about time her parents did something to find her. 'You should call the police anyway. Whether the hand is there or not, I saw it, and they will want to check if Alma really has disappeared.'

. . .

A short time later, I hear Tara calling my name.

'Maria has made you a cup of tea and a bite to eat. Max told me what you've been through. It must have been a dreadful ordeal, and to escape like you did takes guts. Max has taken a look and doesn't know how you managed to get that manacle off your wrist.'

I haul myself into a sitting position, take the mug of tea and plate of cheese on toast from her.

'It wasn't easy, and it hurt like hell,' I tell her. 'Has Max said anything else?'

'Yes, he did, and he called the police. Max says they'll be here shortly and will want to speak to you.'

They'll want to know what I was doing in the pig shed in the first place. They'll see for themselves that it had to be down to Max; there is no alternative.

'Max has agreed that the pigs have to go. I'm not sorry; Hanna won't be either when she returns. The things have been a blot on our lovely garden for long enough.'

'Have you heard from Hanna?'

'No, and it's not like her to disappear like this. In the past I've known where she was, her old room or the pig shed, but this time it's different. She's left us and I've no idea where she would go.'

'Would she go to a friend's house?'

'She's on nodding terms only with people in this village. I've never heard her talk about anyone, and no one has called at the house asking for her. I'm worried about her; this is out of character. I have a feeling she may have left us for good.'

THIRTY-SEVEN

The doctor was right about the good night's sleep. I wake up the following morning feeling fine. Well, apart from a slight headache, which I can live with. I have my usual shower, get dressed and leave for the office.

I find Max sitting at my desk, computer booted and going through the accounts files.

'An Inspector Scott wants a word with you'—he smiles at me—'about yesterday and what you found.'

'What about who locked me in? Can he help with that one?'

'Forensics have had a look around but both the pig pen and shed are not the best places to look for evidence for obvious reasons. They say that any chance of getting fingerprints or DNA is minimal.'

Of course it is, and how convenient. I'm looking at Max sitting behind my desk, and the doubts are back, and I mean seriously back. I've been over this in my head several times and concluded that it had to be him. He can deny it all he wants, but who else is there?

'Did you know this woman, Alma?' he asks, leaving me

thinking of an answer. I don't want to tell him she was my mother or he'll think I was party to the blackmail.

I shake my head and shrug. 'I don't think so, I don't recognise the name.'

'I ask because you were seen drinking coffee with her the other day.'

It's no use denying it, he knows I've lied. He'll want to know why, what we spoke about and think I'm up to something when I refuse to tell him.

'Who saw us?'

'Isabel.'

Not Nicco then, and that surprises me. As for it being Isabel, that damn woman has been at my back since I got here. She was the cause of Hanna's disappearance; had she not come to the house that night, things would have been different.

'Okay, I did speak to Alma.'

'About me?'

I nod. 'You were mentioned.'

'In what context, anything to do with my business?'

'No, we talked about why she was blackmailing you.'

That struck a chord, his face pales and he gets to his feet. Now I've done it, I know the man is dangerous, so why can't I keep my big mouth shut instead of goading him.

'That's nonsense. She can only blackmail me if I've done something wrong, but I haven't. Whatever she told you is rubbish. She's trying her luck, that's all.'

'I think you're wrong; she does know something about you, and I think that's why she came to the house. What does she have on you, Max? It must be something juicy, or you wouldn't have killed her.'

I don't know where that came from but it is the truth. However, blurting it out like that wasn't clever. I don't like the look on his face either; he's trying hard not to lash out. But despite the anger on his face, I can't stop myself.

'I think it goes something like this. Alma blackmails you, and we both know what for, don't we, Max?' I give him a knowing smile but there's no reaction. 'You don't pay up, she threatens to go public, so you kill her. How about that for a theory? D'you think Inspector Scott will go for it?'

I've just played my hand and have nothing more. I hope it's enough for him to leave me alone from now on.

'Okay, Donna, you're well informed. Tell me, why was she blackmailing me?'

He sits there, anger gone and with a smug look on his face. He thinks I don't know, that I'm bluffing, but he's wrong, as he'll soon find out.

'The baby, Max.' The smug face is instantly gone to be replaced by doubt and concern. I've found the sensitive button. 'The one you bought with money, the infant who grew up to be Hanna.' I say no more, certainly not that I know Hanna's *true* identity.

I've never seen such a worried look on his face before. He's shell-shocked; I know the secret he's kept all these years and I can see the cogs turning as he tries to work out how.

Having said my piece, I leave him to stew. I've given him something to think about and I will use it if he ever gets heavy with me again. The man is dangerous and a threat to my safety. I tell the inspector what I know, and they will take him in for questioning. He has a motive for wanting Alma dead, and they can't ignore that.

I need fresh air; the atmosphere in the house is claustrophobic. My spat with Max hasn't helped. I'm a fool to myself, I need to keep my mouth shut and not court trouble. A walk round the village should clear my head.

The village is busy; there is a market on and lots of colourful stalls are strung out along the high street. I wander from one to the other, looking at the variety of things on sale, everything from fruit to jewellery and clothing.

Despite the dozens of people crowding the narrow street, I have the feeling that I'm being followed. Given my history these last three years, it's something I've honed to perfection. I turn round but can't see anyone I recognise. This is a case of imagination in overdrive. Calm down, I tell myself, who'd want to follow me? Even so, I've still got shivers slipping down my back.

'Have you missed me?' a familiar voice asks from behind my back.

'Hanna.' I hug her tight. 'Where have you been? I've been going out of my mind with worry imagining all sorts.'

'I suppose Tara told you a pack of lies, said I was with a friend and enjoying myself?'

'Were you? Why didn't you call me, tell me you were fine?'

Hanna shrugs and shakes her head. 'Didn't think anyone was interested. Certainly not Max and Tara, and you've got enough on your plate.'

'Yes, but a quick call would have done no harm, and it would have reassured me that you were alright.'

'Didn't know you cared,' she says, grinning.

'Come on then, what happened to you.'

'I stayed with a friend. I needed a few days to think, away from the horror that is my family.'

I could do with that myself. But there's things about Hanna's explanation that aren't right. Both Hanna and Tara told me she had no friends; well, no one close enough to stay with for a couple of days.

'Have you been scouting round looking for premises you want to rent?'

'I had another look at the one I like and I've gone for it. I've got the money now to make a start. The unit is great and there is room for a small flat at the back. The minute I've got it liveable, I shall be moving in.'

There was a time when I was doubtful about her ability to cope on her own but not anymore. If she can organise the finance she needs for her business then she's more than capable of taking care of herself. I'm pleased for her. If Alma was right, she's my flesh and blood, young and brave. She deserves to do well.

'Is the funding coming from your dad or has the bank agreed to back you?'

'Max,' she scoffed. 'He wouldn't give me the time of day. No, the bank finally saw sense and coughed up.'

I'm pleased for her; this is just the break she needs.

'Are you coming home later?'

I will feel better once Hanna is where I can both see and speak to her.

'Yes, it's about time I showed my face.'

'You must show me your premises sometime.' I smile at her.

'My life has turned all rosy but you've had it rough; he put you in with the pigs,' she says.

'It was one of the worst experiences of my life,' I admit. 'I thought I was going to die in there, alone, cold and hungry.'

'If you had, there would have been little evidence. The pigs would have eaten you. Horrific, yes, but it has happened before. A pig breeder once told me about a case in Scotland; all that was left of the poor victim was his false teeth. Just as well you escaped; that must have taken some doing.'

Listening to that gruesome story has done nothing for my delicate stomach. But Hanna is right, I have had a lucky escape.

'My thin wrists are responsible for me getting free.'

She holds out one of her fat arms. 'I stood no chance with these, in that case. It's horrendous in that place. I know exactly how you must have felt. Me and that manacle are old friends.'

What to say... to be honest, I haven't the words. To throw your own daughter in that awful place is the act of a man with no heart.

'You must have been as terrified as I was.'

'I thought I'd die in there. Three days, Donna, three days with no food or light, little sleep and only the stench of pig for company.'

'Did you tell Tara?'

'What use is she? The woman has no influence over Max; he does as he pleases. I could have died in that shed and Tara would find some reason to protect him.'

Hanna isn't wrong; Tara needs to realise what's going on and finally stand up to him and put a stop to all of the abuse.

'Do you know about the murder, the body part I found in the pig shed?' I meant to say pen and am about to correct myself when Hanna pulls me into an alleyway.

'That would be Alma,' she whispers.

'You know her?' I'm surprised, the only way that is possible is if Alma contacted her or Nancy told her.

'I knew her well enough to know that she's the one who's been blackmailing Max.' She grins at me. 'He has to have killed her and put her body outside by the shed wall so the pigs would find her.'

That's too gruesome for me to comment.

'Now she's dead, I see no reason why I shouldn't blackmail Max myself.'

'That's a dangerous game to play,' I tell her.

'As long as he doesn't find out it's me, I'll be fine. Alma knew Nancy, did you know that?'

If only she knew. What a conversation that would be.

'The two of them spoke on the phone sometimes. Nancy didn't like her. She told me the woman was evil, and now that she had her claws into her, Alma wouldn't leave her alone.'

Nancy didn't reveal that she was Alma's sister, probably wise of her.

'What is it she had on Max?' I have to find out if Hanna knows the truth of her birth, if Alma told her.

'I'm not telling you.'

Straight to the point, but why so secretive?

'Is it something to do with the business?' I know damn well it isn't, but I don't want Hanna to think I know anything different just yet.

'No, something personal, and I'm not saying anything more, not until he pays up. You know how evil he is; Max deserves everything that's coming to him. He doesn't know I'm the blackmailer and I'll make sure he never finds out, so don't you dare tell him.'

THIRTY-EIGHT

I leave Hanna at the market and make my way back to the house. I've got plenty of things of my own to do. I want answers to the questions that have plagued me since I got the funeral invitation. Opening that damn box might help, and so might cracking the password on those two documents on the memory stick.

As I walk back, I try to work out if Hanna knows that the infant who was sold is her. Then there is the question of how Alma found out where Hanna lived. I have to presume Nancy told her, but why she'd do that is anyone's guess. Nancy didn't like Alma any more than the rest of us. She certainly didn't trust her.

Max and Tara buy a child and raise her as their own. Twenty-three years later, Alma turns up and demands hush money. Nancy must have told her; during the phone calls Hanna mentioned, Nancy must have let something slip. But that in turn begs the question, how did Nancy find out where Hanna was? She must have done her research, but where you'd go to find out about a child who's been sold, I have no idea. My head is full to bursting with questions and possible solutions. I have to let this drop for the time being, at least.

Back at the house I go straight to my rooms. I boot up my laptop and get comfortable. One folder and two documents are what I see on screen. The folder, no problem, I've looked at the contents already, and I'm toying with the notion of deleting them all. If I do, I'll never see them again. I've almost convinced myself that's what I want, but the fact that they are my family, for good or for bad, is what is stopping me.

One more look and then I'll make my mind up. One of the images shows Alma, a couple of the kids from next door and Nancy standing in front of the back door. Nancy is apart from the others right in front of the door. She'd be trying to hide the state the door's in, the flaky paintwork, the lock hanging off and the gap in the wood where a neighbour tried to kick it in. The way we lived embarrassed her. She was the only one in my family who wanted the house doing up, to make it a decent place to live in instead of a hovel.

She never got anywhere; my mother didn't see the point. The day I ran away, Nancy came to blows with my mother over it. That's my last memory; it sums up my life back then perfectly.

Nancy was always the optimist of the family. I wonder if she ever got her way, if the house got the makeover she wanted. I doubt it. Money was always short, so spending it on the house was out of the question.

I've decided that too much reminiscing isn't good for me. Once this is over I won't just delete the photos, I'll destroy the memory stick altogether. But for now, it's the two documents that need my attention. Both are named and password-protected, but why? What's in them that's so secret that Nancy didn't want anyone else to see them?

It's guess the password time again. I was pretty useless last time but I did get there in the end. Think logically, you can do this, says the little voice in my head, but it's wrong; this is hard and I'm lost.

Document one is named *Lucy* and document two, *receipt*. Lucy is Hanna's birth name, the name Nancy gave to her. I've worked out most of the puzzle, thanks to Alma. Nancy came here to find Hanna, or Lucy as she knew her. I guess she took my name because Max wouldn't recognise it. Both Nancy and Alma have the surname Williams, their maiden name. Nancy never married, but Alma was briefly wed to my waster of a father, Jack Anderson. After three months of marriage, he left and we never ever saw him again, so Alma reverted to her maiden name. My birth had been registered, and, knowing her, she wouldn't waste money changing it by deed poll. No one knew who Hanna's father was.

The password for the memory stick was my new name. Is this the key to the documents too? Will my name work for the rest? The first document has the name Lucy. I key in my name just like with the stick itself, nothing. I'm disappointed but not ready to give up, not yet. The answer is here somewhere; I just have to find it.

One swig of water later, I look at the screen again. Lucy Williams is Hanna's real full name. I key it in and hold my breath; much to my relief it works. I hope this is worth waiting for.

It is, it's the birth certificate for Lucy Williams. It's what I would expect. The surname, the address of the hovel where we all lived. And, not surprisingly, no father mentioned. No surprises there. I knew about the affair Nancy had, Alma saw to that. Next, the document named *receipt*.

This one is much trickier. I think it's going to be the receipt that Max gave Alma when he bought Hanna. I still can't believe that he bought a baby.

He paid Alma ten thousand pounds and walked away with Nancy's child. The receipt actually states *for the sale of Lucy*

Williams to Max Marsden. I can only presume that Alma insisted on having this, and Max, being so desperate, gave in to her demands. I can't even begin to guess how Nancy got her hands on it. But is it genuine, or something Nancy put together herself? Should I put it to the test by going to the police and would anyone thank me if I did?

Not Max and Tara for sure, but Hanna might. She'd have a new identity and, as I know, that can be useful. Before I do anything, I'll think it over, weigh up the pros and cons.

Research over and most of my questions answered, I wander downstairs, planning to go out into the garden. But Tara calls to me from the sitting room.

'Where are you going?' she asks.

'For a walk round the garden, that's all. I'll have a look at the flower beds and get some sun. I need to clear my head.'

'Never mind all that boring stuff, come and keep me company instead. I've not seen anyone all day. Max has deserted me and, as for Hanna, well, who knows?'

I'm not keen; I don't fancy conversation right now and especially not with Tara.

'Come on, I think we need to talk about what's been going on these past few days.'

Tara is on the sofa, a gin and tonic in her hand. I get a half-hearted wave, then she holds up her glass.

'There's plenty if you want some,' she calls.

'It's not yet lunchtime; do you think drinking at this time is helping you?'

'Don't question my drinking, Donna,' she snaps back. 'You don't understand, you don't have to live my life. In this house, with that man.'

She starts weeping and grabs my hand. I'm no good in a situation like this. Stand up for yourself is my thing, not dissolving into tears at the first sign of trouble.

'Will you get a fleece jacket from my wardrobe, and I'll

come for a walk outside with you? I get so down, Donna. All this with that woman and the pigs, Hanna disappearing like that... it all plays on my nerves.'

'You'll be fine, you just need to take a deep breath and think about what you want from life.'

I leave her to it and go in search of the fleece. First I've been given the key to the safe and now I've got permission to rifle through Tara's wardrobe. I'm surprised I'm allowed anywhere near it after the thing with the dress.

Through the door, past the en suite where I nearly killed Max, then into a side room which holds an enormous wardrobe. I want to get this over with, I feel nervous being in here.

Tara has at least six fleece jackets hanging up. I grab the black one; she can't complain, it'll go with anything. I'm in a hurry but I can't help a quick peek at the shoe rack on the bottom of the wardrobe. She has shoes to drool over, particularly a pair of ultra-high stilettoes in red patent leather. Tara must have small feet, the shoes are tiny, far too small for me or I'd try them on.

Reluctantly I put them back, move some of the shoe boxes around to see what else she's got lying on the wardrobe floor. It's just the usual stuff, handbags, leather belts and the odd scarf. She's obviously not particularly careful with her things.

One of the larger shoe boxes rattles. I lift the lid to look inside and see baby things. Rattles, a teething ring, and a tiny Babygro, they must have been Hanna's, keepsakes that Tara won't part with. But the item that interests me the most is the small pink blanket. I recognise it; it's the one I bought many years ago when I first heard that Nancy had given birth to a baby girl. It must have been with Hanna when Max took her, and Tara has kept it all this time. More proof if I needed it that Hanna is Nancy's child.

But that's not everything in the box.

Underneath the Babygro, I find an EpiPen.

THIRTY-NINE

I did not expect this. Apart from me, there are three people in this house, and the last person I suspect of having anything to do with what's gone on is Tara. On the night Nancy died, she needed her EpiPen, and it looks like someone deliberately hid it from her. Did Tara hide it from her in her moment of need?

Grabbing the pen and the fleece, I go downstairs to face her. I'm fed up of trying to work out what's going on here. It's about time I got some answers and got the hell away from them all.

'What's this doing in a shoe box in your wardrobe?' I fly at her waving the pen in front of her face. 'You knew how important it was for Nancy to always have it with her, but you hid it. That makes you responsible for her death.'

Her face reddens and she tries to grab the thing off me.

'You're wrong. Last I saw that, it was on the dressing table in Alice's room.' She looks at me, her eyes full of questions, just how I felt when I first got here.

'You just said Nancy had to always have it with her... who is Nancy?'

It's too late to backtrack now, I've slipped up because I was so angry. I need to calm down before I get myself into any more trouble.

'Alice Anderson's real name was Nancy Williams. I'm surprised you didn't know. What surprises me more is why you'd want her dead.'

'I didn't,' she insists. 'I have no idea how the pen got in my wardrobe, and that's the truth.'

She doesn't look guilty, she just looks confused. Perhaps I've made a mistake and Tara isn't to blame and another member of this weird family is trying to frame her.

'Why did Alice use a different name? Why couldn't she just tell us who she was?'

'What's going on?' a voice bellows from behind me. 'You've got Tara in tears, why?'

It's Max. I hold up the EpiPen and wave it at him. 'This was in Tara's wardrobe. You know what that means, Max. Either she's a murderer or someone is trying to set her up.'

Max looks angry. He takes hold of Tara's arm and pulls her to her feet.

'Is what happened to Alice down to you?'

'No,' she shouts at him. 'And Donna has just told me that Alice wasn't her name, that it was Nancy.'

'What are you talking about?' he asks, pushing her back onto the sofa. 'I've no idea what's going on here. I'm still reeling from seeing that hand in the pig pen.'

Confused Max, that's one version I haven't seen. If Tara didn't hide the EpiPen, and Max didn't, that only leaves Hanna. But she got on with Nancy, she liked her, they spent time together, besides which she has no motive.

'I'm keeping this.' I hold the pen in the air again. 'It's evidence, so I'll put it somewhere safe. This means Nancy's death is suspicious, and that shouldn't surprise anyone here.'

'Why?' Tara asks. 'We've done nothing. And why did Alice use a different name? I don't understand.'

Time for an explanation.

'Nancy and Alma were sisters. Nancy came here to work and used a false name, Alice Anderson, because she thought you, Max, might recognise her real one,' I say, taking in Max's face as he slowly realises who Nancy really was.

'Why would he?' Tara asks, still completely in the dark.

If Tara thought about it, I'm sure she would work it all out. She must know that Hanna didn't just appear out of thin air, that getting her in the first place cannot have been done through legal channels. It's time to give the woman a clue.

'Alice, or rather Nancy Williams, is Hanna's birth mother. She came here to find her daughter.'

There, it's said, out in the open where it should be. Mind you, I haven't told them about my name, I'm saving that one for another time.

'Interesting story,' says a voice from behind me. 'But how much of it is true?'

It's Hanna.

'You're back.' Tara smiles and holds out open arms. 'I've missed you. Me and your dad were worried sick. We'd no idea where you were or if anything had happened to you.'

Now it's Hanna's turn to look confused.

'Don't come with the affection now, it's far too late. Neither of you give a shit about me, and that's the truth. I'm sure if that witch Alma would have had me, you would have given me back.'

She knows, Alma must have told her. I bet she didn't do it kindly either. Hearing the truth from a woman like Alma must have upset Hanna, and she didn't deserve that.

'Sit down, Hanna, you're tired and hungry. I'll get Maria to get you some food.'

'You don't do the concerned mother bit well, Tara, so don't even try. I don't want food and I don't want to rest. What I do want is rid of you lot.'

I know Hanna doesn't think much of her parents and is sure they don't think much of her either, but this sort of talk will not solve anything.

'Your parents have been every bit as worried about you as me, Hanna.'

She points at Max. 'He wants me gone. That night he took me outside he gave me a right mouthful. You didn't hear him, raving he was. It is no wonder I took off. I was scared, you know what he's like, Donna, look what he did to you.'

True enough, when he's angry, Max is one scary man. He doesn't look too pleased at the moment either. He's stood by the sitting room door with a frown on his face and his eyes intent on Hanna.

'What exactly did I do to Donna?' he asks her.

'You hit her across the head and locked her in the pig shed.'

Tara gasps and turns her attention to Max.

'Tell me you didn't,' she snaps at him.

'No, I didn't, she's mistaken. I would never do that, it's lies.' Now he's looking at me. 'Did you see who hit you, Donna? Did they give any clue who they were?'

FORTY

Max is right. I presumed it was him because of everything that had happened, that and the fact that I believe him to be capable of anything. But if not him, then who?

'He would say it wasn't him, wouldn't he? Always ready with an excuse is Max.'

Hanna's off and running now, and I can feel her anger. She's standing her ground, and against Max that isn't easy.

'It's not an excuse, it's the truth. I did not assault Donna and I certainly didn't lock her up.'

He turns his attention to me.

'Are you sure you don't know who hit you, Donna?'

'No, how could I? It was dark and I was hit from behind. The last thing I recall is the sound of feet squelching across the pen. I didn't even have time to turn round.'

'In that case you've no proof it was me. It could quite easily have been anyone.'

He's right. I've been so intent on blaming Max for everything that's happened I've not given much thought to the culprit being anyone else. If Max is telling the truth then I'll have to think again.

'And I'm not responsible for the death of that woman Alma either. I have no idea how she ended up in the pig pen, but it had nothing to do with me.'

'Someone put her in there,' Hanna says. 'It has a high fence around it, and the hand was found close to the shed, several metres away from any of the fences,' she continues.

Max is nodding. 'The poor woman was either injured or dead when she was left against the shed wall, and that doesn't happen by accident.'

'You think someone deliberately put her there for the pigs to...'

Tara can't finish the sentence, and no wonder; what happened to Alma is horrific.

My heart pounds as I take in what Hanna just said. There's something else too. When we met in the market, she knew I'd been locked in the pig shed. She hadn't spoken to her family and could not have known that either.

'Hanna, how do you know where the hand was found?'

'You told me when we met in the market.'

'That's not true, I said nothing about where she was found.'

'You must have done, otherwise how would I know?'

How indeed. Nancy, Alma and me if I'd not been so hell-bent on getting out of the pig shed. I've blamed Max for it all, but what if it wasn't him? There is no evidence that he's guilty of any of it. All I've had to go on is the way he treats me and his family, his controlling ways and unreasonable behaviour. But I have to admit that doesn't make him a murderer.

She knows, I can see it in those piercing blue eyes of hers. Hanna knows that I've twigged. But can I prove any of it?

I hold the EpiPen up between my fingers. 'I found this today, hidden where Nancy wouldn't find it.'

'You don't know that. It means nothing.' Hanna shrugs. 'Nancy lost it; she shouldn't have been so careless.'

'I don't think she was, I think this was taken on purpose and hidden from her. It is possible she was deliberately fed the cake that killed her too. I'm sure the police will find out how that happened.'

Hanna doesn't look pleased. She looks from one of us to the other before settling on Max.

'He killed Nancy and the others. He was being blackmailed by Alma, Nancy's sister. Nancy will have helped her.'

'Blackmail? For what? What's he done?' Tara asks.

'Both Alma and Nancy knew that you pair bought me. He had to get rid of them, he can't allow that to come out.'

'You were adopted,' Tara tells her. 'Nobody *bought* you.'

'Alma sold me for ten grand. Ten grand. That's motive enough for everything Max did. Me, what motive do I have? None.'

She's right, I'm swinging to and fro, trying to make up my mind. Motive is everything, people don't murder for no reason.

'Well, someone killed them. Nancy first, then Alma, and I was assaulted and locked up. Then there is this; I found it, Hanna, and know it must have been hidden.'

'You shouldn't go rooting around in Tara's wardrobe, should you? Then we could have avoided all this crap.'

'How do you know that's where it was found, Hanna?'

All eyes turn to look at Hanna. I can see Max is ready to pounce. I was wrong all along, Max is innocent of killing Nancy, certainly... about the others, I'm not sure.

It's at this pivotal moment that the front doorbell rings. Seconds later Maria shows Nicco into the sitting room.

He must sense the atmosphere straight away. He says nothing but looks at us all in turn.

'We're trying to decide who murdered two women,' I tell him. 'We thought Max, but now suspicion has fallen on Hanna.' I sound flippant but that's covering up the nerves and the fact I want to throw up again.

'Max wouldn't kill anyone,' Nicco says, walking into the room as we all turn at his voice, and suddenly his huge frame looks even more menacing.

FORTY-ONE

'You have no idea, have you?' Hanna looks at her parents. 'You two stole me; money changed hands but that's what you did. I hate you both for it and the others who helped. Alma and Nancy both knew and said nothing. You too, Donna, or whatever your real name is.'

This outburst is unexpected and shocks me. I had no idea Hanna felt this way. I would have told her eventually, explained gently what happened, but no, Alma got to her first and filled her head full of lies.

'We wanted you for the best of reasons,' Tara tells her. 'You were the answer to a prayer. We loved you, gave you everything and just wanted you to be happy.'

Tara's words are heartfelt but they have no effect on Hanna. She stands defiant, convinced she's in the right.

'Happy? Don't forget he used to lock me in that room; that's not love, that's hate.'

Max says nothing, he can hardly deny it.

'Nancy, my so-called birth mother, left me with Alma; she sold me for money. Those are the two people I hate even more than you,' she shouts at her parents. 'Nothing you say will change that. I found out the truth off Nancy. She actually thought she was helping. She came to this house to find me. Nancy tried to explain but failed. I put on a good show but I vowed to get even. Selling me to you pair was a bad mistake, and they had to pay for it.'

That's some admission. She hid her feelings well, I never suspected. I didn't think she even knew all this until she just told us.

'And as for you'—she turns those piercing blue eyes on me—'I knew what you were up to right from the start. Nancy and Alma were your family, and you are no better than them.'

She's wrong there. It seems to me my immediate family is split into two camps, the good and the bad. I'd put Nancy and me in the good and most definitely Alma and now Hanna in the bad.

I have no idea where we go from here, but before I have a chance to respond to Hanna, the screech of the doorbell has us all jumping. Max and Tara never have visitors, so who just showed up?

'Detective Inspector Scott,' a middle-aged, overweight man tells us as he enters the room while flashing his warrant badge at us. I catch sight of Maria scurrying back to the kitchen, having answered the door and presumably sensed the tension in the room.

'I'm looking for Max Marsden?'

'That's me.' Max steps forward.

'Mr Marsden, I'm here to talk about the body part that was found in the pig shed. Your pig shed, I believe. We have identified it as belonging to Alma Williams; did you know her?'

'She was my mother,' I tell him.

'And you are?'

'Donna Slade, Mr Marsden's PA.'

Telling him my real name will only confuse matters. The family know me as Donna, so I have no choice but to stick with it for now.

'Williams was known to us, she's been arrested in the past for theft and a minor assault; that's how we were able to match her DNA.'

Alma having a record doesn't surprise me at all. What does surprise me is her not languishing in a prison cell somewhere.

'Your pigs will be taken away, Mr Marsden. They'll be put to sleep and the stomach contents examined.'

Tara looks as if she's about to throw up, but it sounds fair enough to me.

'There have been other serious incidents in this house,' Nicco surprised me by saying. 'Another woman...' He looks at me for a name.

'Nancy Williams,' I say. 'Alma's sister. Nancy's EpiPen was deliberately hidden from her, and she died of anaphylactic shock.'

'Was it reported?'

'No,' Max tells him. 'That fact has only been discovered today.'

Nicco steps forward. 'Before you arrived, the young lady who's stood over there confessed to both murders and to assaulting Donna here.'

'We will need a statement,' Scott says, turning to Hanna.

'I've done nothing, he's lying. It's a plot to move suspicion from Max.'

'Nice try, Hanna,' Nicco says, holding up his mobile, 'but I have it recorded on here.'

Thank god for Nicco and his quick thinking. Hanna isn't impressed. She flies at him, her fists poised to thump him, but is stopped by Scott just in time.

Hanna is led away. I, for one, am relieved, but Tara looks devasted.

'Thanks for that, Nicco. Without your recording we'd have nothing.'

'I like Hanna, but she's always been a strange young woman, a loner and doesn't mix well.'

I could say the same about myself but don't. At some point I will bring Nicco up to speed, tell him all the gory details about my family, but for now I'm sick of talking about them, particularly Alma, who started all this.

'As well as Max Marsden, there's his wife, the daughter, a cook and you living here, is that right?'

'There are things about this that I don't understand.'

Max is curious, he's bound to be, I believed he was a murderer. 'Can explanations wait, Max? I'm not up to a long conversation right now. The police will want to speak to me but that will have to wait too.'

He shrugs and gives me a smile. Nice Max, just when I need him. I nod and leave them to it. My throat's dry and my voice doesn't sound right.

Back in my rooms, I flop on my bed and try to blot out what just happened. I feel sorry for Hanna and for Max and Tara too. The story is bound to get out and they will suffer gossip, and charges could be made against Max for what he did.

Nancy didn't deserve what happened to her. She came here to find her daughter and died because of it. As for Alma, she was my mother, not that I had any affection for her; even so, becoming pig food isn't what I'd have wished for her.

I have two more mysteries to solve and then I'm out of here. First, there's Nancy's old box and the letter, and second, the email that brought me here in the first place. Hanna denies having anything to do with it, and it's unlikely to be down to either Max or Tara either.

I decide to tackle the box. I reckoned I needed a hammer and chisel but with luck I'll figure out the proper sequence this time.

But I don't, and the thing is just as difficult as last time. I'm at my wits end with it. I won't be thwarted by an old wooden box. Grabbing the box in anger, I throw it against the wall. Stupid, I know, if either Max or Tara hear the noise they'll come looking. Despite that, my show of frustration is worth it: one of the sides breaks off, revealing the secret compartment and out falls the letter.

Tearing at the envelope I pull out a sheet of pink notepaper smelling of violets. I recognise it at once: Nancy wrote on paper exactly like this. Violets were her thing; everything she had stunk of them. As a child the smell made me feel sick.

It's dated the week before she died. She writes about finding out about Hanna, or Lucy as she knew her. How she didn't want to give her up but had no choice when she was hospitalised. She never forgave Alma for what she did and spent most of her adult life trying to find out where Lucy was. It was Alma who told her and about her scheme to blackmail Max. Nancy got the job here and tried to mend her relationship with Lucy.

It didn't work, Nancy planned to give up the job and get back to her own life. Lucy, she writes, was a lost cause. Nancy has a will, and I am the sole beneficiary. If anything happens to her, I'm to have the money in her bank account. Written in the final paragraph is the name of her solicitor.

I have tears running down my cheeks as I take it all in. There's nothing written in the letter that I don't already know, but it's a link to her and one I'll always treasure.

Now for the mystery of the email. I've no idea how to solve that one.

FORTY-TWO

The following morning, I ask both Max and Tara about the email, but they assure me that they know nothing about it, and I believe them. They have no reason to lie. I also tell them about my name change and the money I owe to the man who has been hunting me ever since.

'Why, Donna, why not go to the police and tell them you were hounded by that villain?'

'That villain, as you call him, has people everywhere. I wouldn't have survived. A change of name was the only thing I could do.'

'And you've lived like a recluse for the last three years?'

I can see Max is having a problem believing this. I'm talking about a world he has no experience of.

'Yes, I have lived in the shadows; my only friend, the only person I confided in, was Ella, the girl who let me stay with her when my landlord threw me out of the bedsit I rented.'

'That's some life you've led. It would break most people.'

'It nearly broke me; I'd no idea I had such resilience until it was needed.'

'The email, why is it so important?'

'Because I don't know who sent it to me. Whoever it was knew my new name, my email address and likely that I'd known Nancy. As you already know Nancy had taken my name. Can you imagine the horror I felt when I saw my real name, Alice Anderson, on the coffin? You had no idea, but you did help. Taking control, giving me a lift to the wake. I'd have been lost without you.'

'You still don't like me much though, do you? I know we have had our moments, but I'm not going to apologise, Donna. I am not perfect but I'm not a murderer.'

That still doesn't excuse the way he has treated me and those around him. He's a strange mix, difficult to take to on one hand but charming on the other.

'Are you planning to leave us?'

'When I've solved the email thing.'

'Will you still be Donna?'

'No, I think I've had enough of being Donna. I'm going to go back to being Alice, it's about time.'

It's another nice day so I take a walk around the village before I go back and start to pack away my stuff. Knowing who sent me the email is important, but I have to face facts, I might never find out.

This time there will be no ghosts waiting for me, no one waiting to fill my head with stuff to rot my brain. I wander round the park, take a look inside the huge Victorian greenhouse and look at the exotic plants. A river cuts the park in two with a series of flat stepping stones to walk across. Children are playing on them, jumping from one to another. This is a glorious place to live, but even with the money Nancy left me, I still can't afford to buy property here.

It's at this point, my mind more settled and the mystery

almost done, that I have an idea. Nicco knew Andrew Wolfenden, the man I owed money too; perhaps he can help me with the email puzzle. I figure that if no one in the Marsden household sent it then it had to be an outsider.

I give him a ring, tell him where I am and wait in the café.

'You're looking better. It'll be a load off your mind to have the truth out in the open.' I give him a quizzical look. 'Max rang me; he's in a state, I'm afraid.'

'I can't comment on that, Nicco. Max is complicated and at times hard to stomach. But that's not why I want to see you. I came here to attend a funeral, the invite was emailed to me. Simple enough, a day's outing and then it's over. But that's not what happened. I fell headlong into a mystery, one I couldn't solve, which has dragged up memories I'd have preferred to stay buried.'

'You think I can help?'

'I've dealt with the mystery, Nicco, but I've got one more thing to sort and then I'm out of here. I've lived under the Marsden roof for long enough.'

'They aren't easy, I know that from years of experience. What's this *thing* that's bugging you?'

I might as well tell him; I've nothing to lose. 'It was the email that invited me to the funeral, I don't know who sent it. Whoever it was knew things about me known only to a handful of people. I thought it must be someone from the Marsden house but apparently not. None of them know anything about it. I don't like mysteries, and for me, this has been the king of them all. It's the one thing that's kept me here, but it's time to leave now, and it looks like I'll have to give up on the email.'

'That's a shame,' Nicco says. 'Solving the mystery means a lot to you. You're right, perhaps I can help.'

'I'm sorry to bother you with this; to be honest, I'm clutching at straws. You can't possibly know the answer.'

'That's where you're wrong, Alice. I can give you the answer to your little puzzle right now.'

He called me Alice, the first person here who has.

'Go on then, who sent the email?'

'I did.'

EPILOGUE

I never thought there would ever be peace in this house but I was wrong. The past week has been heaven. There's no longer any office work to do; Tara has kept herself to herself, and the police organised the removal of the pigs.

I made my statement to the police and DI Scott seemed happy with it, which is a relief. I know nothing about what's happened to Hanna. Max and Tara have visited her but she refused to speak to them. At the initial hearing she didn't get bail and blamed them both.

As for me, I've got over what Nicco told me. I'd never have guessed in a million years. He wouldn't tell me anything else that day, he said he had some stuff to sort out; I'm seeing him later tonight to explain. He's taking me to Lakeside for dinner. It's not a date or anything, just an opportunity to talk things over in different surroundings. Tara has given me a lovely apple-green dress to keep, the perfect colour given my red hair, she said. She had a smile on her face at the time, so I'm honoured.

I'm not sure what I feel for Nicco. He's an odd one; I think it's his size that does it. He seems willing to help me but I mustn't forget that he bought the outstanding customer debts off Wolfenden, mine among them. He's sent a taxi for me and on the way to the restaurant I try to make up my mind.

He's waiting for me in the foyer, takes my hand and leads the way to our table. The soft lighting makes a difference, makes him seem less intimidating.

'Do you remember what I told you at the wake?' He begins as he pours the wine.

Here it comes, he wants to talk about the money I now owe him. 'You told me lots of things but I'd had a shock, the coffin and all that, so I don't recall much.'

'I told you about Andrew Wolfenden.'

My stomach does a somersault; this isn't what I was expecting.

'I told you that Wolf was ill, retired from the money-lending business and living in Spain.'

I nod, I do remember that much.

'I also told you that he'd sold on the debts that people owed him.'

I don't know where this is going but I'm not happy. I thought Nicco was a friend but now I'm not so sure.

'I bought some of those debts,' he all but whispers. 'Among them yours, Alice.'

Great, I don't owe Wolfenden anymore but this hunk of muscle.

'What d'you intend to do about it?'

'Nothing at all. As far as I'm concerned, the debt is wiped clean.' He winks at me. 'You don't know it, but you should know that Wolf was aware of your name change. He also knew about Nancy and her job. He would have used that information against you.'

'That doesn't explain why you bought my debt and now want to cancel it out.'

'I'm close to the Marsden family. I knew that there was something odd about how they got Hanna; there was no adoption, so whatever happened cannot have been legal. Wolf had dealings with Alma; she told him your new name, where Nancy was and that you'd no doubt contact her sooner or later. Inevitably, if Wolf upset the way things were, that would mean trouble for Max. He's a wealthy man and given the way he got Hanna that made him a sitting duck. Trouble for Max means trouble for me. I'm his accountant but I do have a share in the business. It folds, and we're both in trouble. I wanted Wolf out of our lives, and that meant removing your family from his clutches. When Wolf fell ill one way of doing that was buying your debt and Alma's from him. When Nancy died I thought you should know. I was aware of your new name but I didn't know that Nancy had taken yours. Her motivation? Protection from Max, he would have recognised her real one.'

That is the last part of my mystery solved, but what now? Nicco has a hold over me rather than Wolf; that should make me happy but I can't make up my mind.

'Thank you, Nicco, but you should have told me before now. Before the funeral would have been helpful. I would have liked to know who I was mourning.'

'Sorry, I could only make it to the wake. If I'd made the actual funeral I would have taken you to one side. But, as it was, Max had taken you under his wing, so I let things be.'

'What now?'

'You go back to your life, and I continue with mine.'

That makes me feel strangely flat. The mystery, the Marsden family have filled my entire life recently. The idea of returning to my own doesn't appeal. But I'm forgetting Nancy's money; that will help me make a fresh start.

'What's your full name? Nicco must be short for something.'

'Nicolas Baxter, but since I was a child, it's always been Nicco. Once you leave the Marsden household and find yourself between places to live, I have a spare bedroom you're welcome to.'

He has a smile on his face, not as charming as that of Max Marsden but kinder somehow. I give him a smile back and nod my head.

'Thanks, that's a generous offer.'

Two Weeks Later

Two weeks have passed since I had dinner with Nicco at the Lakeside restaurant. I thought about it, but in the end I didn't take him up on the offer of his spare room. He's a pleasant and surprisingly kind man but I do not want him to get the wrong impression. I am definitely not looking for any sort of relationship yet and don't want him thinking otherwise.

The rawness of recent events is slowly diminishing. I have no choice but to accept what has happened to Hanna. I'll wait until after her trial and then I'll visit her. She has done some dreadful things but she is the only blood relative I have left, and I would like to have some sort of relationship with her. Despite her complete lack of affection for any of her family, I also regret what happened to Alma and that we didn't make our peace.

I'm making one last visit to the Marsden house and I am nervous. I have no idea what sort of reception I'll get. I wouldn't bother, but I still have some of my stuff to pick up before I leave them and this pretty little village for good. As I walk up the driveway, my thoughts turn to Nancy. I wish I could have seen her, had one last conversation and thanked her for the money she left me. I smile to myself. I might even have given her a piece of my mind for the mystery I had to unravel. Her money will help me make a fresh start, something I should be looking forward to, so why do I feel so flat? Financial stability is all very well, but I also need a purpose; a job I can get my teeth into would do it.

I ring the front doorbell, and Tara answers. She looks perfect as usual except for a pair of thick gardening gloves that are no doubt protecting those expensive fingernails of hers.

'Alice, how lovely to see you.' She leans forward and gives me a peck on the cheek. 'It's a first, but I'm about to help Mervyn, my gardener, prune the roses.' She nods at an elderly man stood behind her, wielding a pair of secateurs. 'Max will be delighted that you've come. He's spoken about you a great deal since you left.'

I can't think why; after all, I blew his world apart.

'Max is in the office, go up and say hello.'

All I want to do is grab my stuff and leave, but what choice do I have? I don't want to appear rude or upset Tara. The decision is taken out of my hands as Max bounds down the stairs and gives me one of his special smiles and a hug.

'I'm glad you've come to see us, Alice; despite all that's happened, I didn't want you to simply fade from our lives.'

He means it, the expression on his face tells me that.

'You don't have to leave us, you know,' he says. 'Your job and accommodation are still here if you want them.'

That is an offer I didn't expect, and it's thrown me; should I take him up on it? The truth is I don't know, and it's not a decision I can make on the spur of the moment.

'Think about it, take a day or two and then we can talk again.'

I hear his office phone ring, I get an encouraging nod, and he's gone.

'Things are as busy as ever, and he does miss you,' Tara assures me. 'Please think carefully about staying with us.'

Now I feel guilty because I haven't missed them; the aggro is gone, and I'm sleeping at night. Although staying at Ella's isn't ideal, she has made me welcome and is a good listener.

I've told her everything that has happened, including about Hanna.

'I will have a think and let you know as soon as possible.' A hug from Tara then I pick up my old sports bag that has been left on the hall table for me and leave. I had intended to have one last look round the village but my mind is in turmoil. Max's offer has thrown me. I'm tossing it about in my mind when a familiar voice calls my name.

Isabel pulls up beside me in her car. She is not my favourite person and I definitely don't want to stand around gossiping with her.

'I thought we'd seen the last of you, but here you are, large as life. For your own sake, I hope you don't intend to stay.'

Still the same Isabel with her jibes and disapproval. 'I'm here to pick up my belongings, nothing more.'

'Sensible and safe, but a word of warning: put as much distance between you and Max Marsden as you can. Hanging around is risky, you know too much.'

'Is that a threat, Isabel? If it is, you are taking on the wrong person.'

Her face falls. 'It's not a threat, Alice, it's a warning, nothing more,' she insists. 'I've finished my relationship with Max for good. I no longer have anything to do with him or his company. I've had all I can take of his unlawful dealings, and I'm still in two minds whether to go to the police or not.'

I'm annoyed; unlike me, Isabel can't simply walk, she has to make trouble, dramatize her exit. 'I have no idea what you're talking about. You and Max are over, and here you are doing your best to make trouble for him.'

'You couldn't be more wrong, believe me, Alice. You have only scratched the surface of Max Marsden's secrets,' she tells me. 'I was close to him, his accountant for many years, and I saw the money that poured into his secret bank account. He wasn't shy about telling me where it came from either.'

I've got better things to do than listen to her. I have no idea what she's talking about anyway and start to walk away.

'Hanna wasn't the only one,' she shouts after me. 'When he bought her, Max spotted an opportunity to make money and went for it.'

An opportunity.

I stand still. I know what's coming next but I don't want to hear her speak the words.

'Max has been buying and selling infants for years.'

I want to tell Isabel that she's lying, simply making trouble, but she's not. There is real fear on her face.

I feel sick, dizzy, and I am trying hard to steady my breathing. Acquiring Hanna the way Max did was one thing, and the only way I can square that one is because I know the kind of life she'd have had if she'd stayed with Alma.

'If you don't believe me, think about it. Where did the start-up money come from when Max first built his little empire? His first project was a small estate of ten detached houses. He needed a fortune to pay for the land, hire builders and buy materials.'

'He will have got a bank loan,' I say, lamely wishing that was true.

'Not the amount he needed. I know the truth, Alice, and so did Nancy. She hated Max for taking her child, but when she discovered the full extent of what he was doing, she was horrified.'

There is passion in her voice and an expression on her face I haven't seen before. This isn't an example of Isabel's spite, she means every word, but what do I do about it? I have no proof and neither does she, but I can't simply walk away and pretend I didn't hear what she has just told me.

The job, living in close proximity to Max and Tara, is one way of getting the proof I need, but I'm torn. 'Is this still going on?'

If her answer is no then I'll walk on, leave this place for ever and not look back. But if Isabel tells me that Max is still knee-deep in this awful trade, then one way or another, I will have to make him stop.

And I know what that means: another clandestine investigation.

A LETTER FROM HELEN

Dear reader,

I want to say a huge thank you for choosing to read *The Funeral*. If you did enjoy it and want to keep up to date with all my latest releases, just sign up at the following link. Your email address will never be shared and you can unsubscribe at any time.

www.bookouture.com/helen-h-durrant

When I started out on this writing journey, I could only dream of reaching readers like you. Your kind words and thoughtful feedback have been a source of inspiration and motivation for me. It is readers like you who make the countless hours of writing, editing and rewriting worthwhile.

I hope you enjoyed *The Funeral*, and if you did, I would be very grateful if you could write a review. I'd love to hear what you think, and it makes such a difference helping new readers to discover one of my books for the first time.

I love hearing from my readers – you can get in touch through social media.

Thanks,

Helen H. Durrant

facebook.com/HelenHDurrantPage

ACKNOWLEDGEMENTS

I want to thank Bookouture for giving me the opportunity to write for them. Special thanks must go to Helen Jenner, who edited the initial manuscript. Helen can have a gold star for her patience and the support she has given me. I don't think I could have completed the book without her.

Thanks to other members of the team, whose contribution is vital to the success of *The Funeral*. Publishing executive: Ria Clare. Publicist: Jess Readett. Copyeditor: Donna Hillyer. Proofreader: Lynne Walker. Cover designer: Lisa Brewster. Audiobook narrator: Sarah Durham.

PUBLISHING TEAM

Turning a manuscript into a book requires the efforts of many people. The publishing team at Bookouture would like to acknowledge everyone who contributed to this publication.

Audio
Alba Proko
Sinead O'Connor
Melissa Tran

Commercial
Lauren Morrissette
Hannah Richmond
Imogen Allport

Cover design
The Brewster Project

Data and analysis
Mark Alder
Mohamed Bussuri

Editorial
Helen Jenner
Ria Clare

Copyeditor
Donna Hillyer

Proofreader
Lynne Walker

Marketing
Alex Crow
Melanie Price
Occy Carr
Cíara Rosney
Martyna Młynarska

Operations and distribution
Marina Valles
Stephanie Straub
Joe Morris

Production
Hannah Snetsinger
Mandy Kullar
Ria Clare
Nadia Michael

Publicity
Kim Nash
Noelle Holten
Jess Readett
Sarah Hardy

Rights and contracts
Peta Nightingale
Richard King
Saidah Graham

Printed in Great Britain
by Amazon

62057812R00143